BIGGEST FAN

DWYM Series:
Biggest Fan
Biggest Regret
The Rebirth

TRIGGER WARNINGS

This story contains content that might be troubling to some readers, including, but not limited to, depictions of and references to suicide, childhood trauma, child abuse, PTSD, murder, rape, stalking, substance abuse, graphic sexual scenes, graphic violence and murder, and strong language.
If any of these content warnings may be a trigger for you as a reader, please do not proceed.

PLAYLIST

Scan QR code to listen:

Apple Music: **Spotify:**

"Save Your Tears" by: Milky Chance
"I'm Not The Only One" by: Sam Smith
"Arsonist's Lullabye" by: Hozier
"Pain and Misery" by: The Teskey Brothers
"Unholy War" by: Jacob Banks
"Bloodstream" by: Stateless
"Boy Got It Bad" by: KaiL Baxley
"Second & Sebring" by: Of Mice & Men
"Think I'm In Love With You" by: Chris Stapleton
"Breathe Me" by: Sia
"Tear you Apart" by: She Wants Revenge
"Falling Away from Me" by: Korn
"Oxytocin" by: Billie Eilish

CHAPTER ONE
CELESTE

I lie with my feet dangling over my best friend's bed as she sits on the floor doing her makeup. "I just need ten minutes." I sigh, staring at the ceiling, which I am pretty sure is growing mold spores. I'll have to google that later. Mold can be yellow, right?

"Girl, you know I can't get you in. My boss knows we are best friends *and* roommates. I'll lose my job if he finds out."

I let out an irritated groan. I've been begging Lily, my best friend, my ride or die, my homegirl, to get me into Club Opal all week. She works there three days a week while going to school and working at a coffee shop, and if I am being completely honest, if it wasn't for me, Lily would forget to eat and breathe. But because she is my *best friend, my ride or die, my home girl,* I make sure she still functions like a human being. Yet, she won't take this one risk for me. I know it's a huge one, I know the rules.

Club Opal is high end, meant for celebrities, rich assholes, yadda yadda. I, on the other hand, am not a celebrity, and am not rich. No. I, Celeste Jones, am a small-town girl who moved to this hell of a city and now work for a small shit-talking magazine company as paparazzi. And since I hate my fucking job—my income is proof—I have to sit here on this mattress in my best friend's room, begging her to get me into this damn club so I can take this damn photo of this stupid fucking celebrity!

"Please, please, please, please, please—"

"I'll kill you," Lily snaps, turning toward me to show her smudged lipstick that I caused by swinging my legs around.

"I'm not going to make rent!" I cry, flipping around so that I'm lying on my stomach watching Lily through the mirror. "Rowan Harper's photos sell for *thousands,* and we both know we need it."

Lily's finger twirls into her shirt, which is a good sign. She is thinking. *Yes, yes, think about it!* But then her emerald eyes squint into fine lines and she smirks. "You don't want the photo. You just want to meet him."

"Ugh!" I roll back over to stare at the mold on her roof, but my view of the fungi is blocked by Lily's face. Her wavy blond hair falls down into my field of vision. "Sorry, babe. I can't risk this job.

Stand outside with the rest of the annoying paparazzi and let me know how it goes."

Oh yeah, because I love standing in the freezing cold with annoying stuck-up men who will stab you over a spot in line. Have you ever seen a female paparazzi? I doubt it. That's why I'm broke. Because I refuse to risk my life over a damn photo. Being a woman in this world is hard enough, but being a woman in a male-saturated industry? Double homicide.

Clothes are now flying into the air as Lily tries to find her apron for work. "Found it! I'm going to be so late again." Lily grabs a chunk of my hair, pulling my head to look at her. "I'm sorry again. But!" She smiles wide, her dimple creating a crater into her cheek. "If you need coffee, you know where to find me," she sings before skipping out the door.

Okay, so plan A is a complete failure. Which forces me to plan B. Not only is it embarrassing to be paparazzi, but it's complete ego death to be a struggling artist. My paintings are not selling like they used to. At first, it was nirvana watching my sales soar to the sky when I first started. Now, I wince every time I open my website to see no orders. I do price my paintings high, because hello! I know my worth. But I can't even get anyone to buy a print. God, and don't even get me started on marketing. The social media algorithm? Yuck.

But since I have no other option—unless I want Lily to pay my half of the rent *again*—I force my little ass up and walk across the house toward my bedroom. I grab my purse, my camera bag, and my keys, and go to the only place where I can get any inspiration.

Central Park is the only location in New York that I find vibrant. I come here to take pictures of random strangers and place myself into their lives—pretend I am in their shoes so I can forget about mine. I come here to take as many photos as I can, as inspiration, then I go home and paint my photos in my own weird, abstract way.

As a scroll through my photos, my face softens with every flick. Nothing is giving me that spark. When I first started painting, I was doing it for myself, for fun—a way to hash out my own emotions with colors, a brush, and a canvas. But now it feels forced and rushed. Rushed to make money off it so I can continue living in the brownstone with Lily. Rushed as I try to keep up with new styles and tricks. Then you add the marketing to it and the socializing, and your hobby is now soiled with the American dream.

I take a deep breath and put my camera back into its bag. I zip up my leather jacket and bundle my chin deeper into my scarf. The wind is high today, which forces water droplets from the fountain to blow my way. I've lived here for a couple of years, but one thing I will never get used to is the damn weather. If I ever did a search on my background, I wouldn't doubt somewhere in my family tree is someone who came from the Caribbean. My tan skin, wide nose, and dark brown eyes are meant for sunny, humid weather. Not what I am currently dealing with in this city.

Before I sulk all the way home about my failures in life, I decide to walk down to Caffee Latte where Lily works. As soon as I walk in, I see my friend behind the counter, twirling her ponytail, hypnotizing the poor businessman at the counter.

When we make eye contact, she jumps in the air, clapping her hands. "Same thing?!"

I nod my head at her and take the first seat at the table near the door. As Lily turns around to make my coffee, I watch the man she was talking to write something on a card and push it down the counter before leaving. I wish I knew how Lily finds the energy to fall into relationships. My best friend is gorgeous, which is obvious, so men will give her anything she wants as long as she bats her eyelashes. But they never last, and every time I ask her what happened to Johnny, Rob, Blake, or Andrew, she waves me off and tells me they were boring.

Lily sits down in the chair across from me and hands me my coffee. "So, what's the plan? Plan A isn't going to work. What's plan B? Should I start putting up signs that my best friend is on the corner of Wilmot Street and she sucks mean dick?"

I put on my gloves so I can grab the frozen salted caramel latte, because I refuse to ever have hot coffee. Something about it makes me squirm in disgust. "How much do you think I should charge for a blow job?"

Lily snorts but gives me her serious face, and I know if she were standing up right now, she would have her hands on her hips like a mom. "C'mon, Celeste. What is the worst that can happen if you stand outside with the rest of the creeps?"

"Creeps?!"

"Oh, you know what I mean."

"Well for starters, someone could step on my toes."

"*Ooo* yeah, you just got your toes done, huh?" Lily taps her index finger on her lips before she snickers. "But you're always in those large, combat curb-stomper boots so you'll be fine." She waves me off, getting out of her seat to help the next customer.

Biggest Fan

As I am about to walk out the door with my bags and coffee, Lily screams at me from across the shop. "At the end of the day, Celeste, I can help you pay the rest of rent!"

I turn around with mortification written across my forehead and everyone in the building staring at me. "Oh yeah, thanks Lil, just let the whole shop know I'm broke!"

A guy sitting at a table near the window snaps his fingers in the air. "Girl, same!"

Lily points to the guy, nodding her head down, and I give her the middle finger as I walk out the door. My life is a complete embarrassment.

Chapter Two
Celeste

Did I already mention that my life is a complete embarrassment? Seriously, if you look up the definition of embarrassment, underneath it will say: Celeste Jones. Because for one, I am standing outside in twenty-five-degree weather. It feels a little warmer because the guy next to me is breathing so hard, it's warming the air around us. Two, I don't even think he knows I am right next to him since I am standing at a good five-foot-three (with the two-inch boots I have on). And three, if you can't tell already, I went with plan B, which is standing outside for over two hours waiting to see if Rowan Harper shows up to Club Opal.

Let's also note that it's 10 p.m., Lily went inside an hour ago, and when she noticed me in the crowd, she pointed me out and waved to me, which resulted in all her friends side-eyeing me.

So, here I stand, outside of this club at the edge of Brooklyn behind red ropes. Waiting for— And here he is! Lights immediately start flashing when the rumble of an all-black Aston Martin

Valkyrie pulls up to the curb. Butterfly doors open and Rowan Harper himself (I'm going to gag) steps out of the driver's side. He's wearing a black button-down shirt and black jeans. He walks smoothly to the passenger side of his vehicle, tucking his chin into his chest to try and avoid the paparazzi taking photos of him, and opens the door for his current supermodel girlfriend (at least, that is what the tabloids are saying she is).

For being the number one bachelor in the city, I expected him to have his own driver. But I'm sure his ego is too big to have someone else drive his precious car. He keeps his hand up, covering his face as he walks down the red carpet, and throws his key to the VIP. When he makes it through the doors, all the lights stop and all the men around me mumble and compare photos.

"Son of a bitch!" Everyone turns to me as I stomp my foot and stare at my camera. Not one photo was taken. I was so focused on the moment, my dumb ass didn't even think of picking up my camera.

I squeeze through the crowd until I can finally breathe my own air. This was my last chance and actually, *my only* chance. I don't know what I was thinking, believing I could paint and sell my art in three days before rent is due, and Lily's option of me being on the corner was never *actually* an option. I'll be damned if I let Lily pay my part of the rent again. She works extremely hard, and it would make me feel like a complete bum if I continued mooching off her.

I walk toward the end of the alley in the back. There are no lights but the red door that is in the middle of the brick wall is pretty inviting. I put my hand on the handle, hesitating. If I get caught entering the club by Lily or her boss, Lily might murder me. And thanks to Lily being so friendly, and pointing me out earlier, all of her coworkers could and would notice me. But maybe if I hide in a corner, in the dark—I've never been inside so I'm hoping it's dark—nobody will see me. And maybe Rowan will walk by and I can get a photo. Then I'm out.

Yep, that's the plan.

I jump on the balls of my feet, puffing air from out my lips to hype myself up. My adrenaline kicks in and I swing the door open hard enough for it to slam against the brick wall.

Standing in the doorway is a humongous and very bald bodyguard. He turns around right when the door opens, freezing me in place. Behind him is a red room with red curtains, red couches, red floors—lots of red. "Falling Away from Me" by Korn blasts throughout the club. My eyes bounce off every inch of the interior until they meet piercing dark eyes.

Biggest Fan

Shit, that's Rowan. My eyes dart to the person sitting next to him, whom I would assume would be the supermodel he came with but instead is a blond-haired man with bright blue eyes. Both of them stare at me with concern.

As I reach for my camera, the man standing in the doorway yells, "Hey! You can't be here!" He reaches out to grab for my camera, and when I realize this is a fight I am going to lose, I turn on my heels and run away.

I dash all the way to my car, which is two blocks away. Once I reach my pretty baby, I place my hands on the hood, taking sharp inhales as I try to catch my breath. "Fuck," I whisper. I shake my head and unlock my 1970 Chevy Chevelle. My heart is pounding in my chest, my lungs burn from inhaling the freezing air, and my feet are aching in my boots.

I sit in my car, turning on the heater and blowing into my gloved hands. I'm not giving up. So if that means waiting here all night for Mr. Harper to stride out of this club, then so be it.

Okay, I'm regretting this. I look at the clock on my dash to read 12:57 a.m. I've parked my car across the street, close enough to watch the club without being noticed. I shift in my seat, trying to get more comfortable. My boss better give me a good check for this. This is torture. I pick up my phone to scroll through social media for the sixth time, but once my page refreshes, the Aston Martin drives past me and pulls to the entrance curb. I throw my phone in the back seat and reach for my camera next to me. As soon as I have my lens in the air, zooming in, Rowan jumps into the car and steps on the gas.

"Mother fucker!" I throw my camera in the passenger seat and put my car in drive. Mr. Harper can hide, but he can't run from me and my Chevy. 450 American horsepower against a foreign vehicle. I don't know how much horsepower a Martin has (I'll have to look that up later,), but that doesn't matter! With the work I've put into this vehicle, I'd beat this butterfly-looking luxury car any day.

I come to a red light behind him and stay at a two-car distance. As soon as the light turns green, he floors it, taking off at a high speed. I smile, biting my lip, and change gears as fast as I can to keep up. I watch him cut into an alley and my heart falls to the pit of my stomach. Does he know I am following him? I slow down to second gear and when I pass the alley, I see his car with his lights off.

I hit the next intersection and make a left turn to cut him off. I turn off my lights and watch him fly through another light. I make a right turn to get behind him, tracking from a large distance for over twenty minutes until we reach a neighborhood. Staying at the entrance, I watch him disappear through a gate.

I quickly pull off the street next to a curb and cut off my engine. I grab my camera and exit the vehicle. I can only see the outline of large mansions as I walk up the community sidewalk. None of the houses have gates, showing their bricked, rocked, and tiled driveways. Some of their entrances have lights, revealing their pristine shrubs. As I pass each house, I try to stare into their vast windows to see what they look like inside.

My breaths become deeper from walking up the hill until I finally reach the only gated house on the block. I hold on to the black metal, trying to catch my breath.

I should have parked fucking closer.

On my left is an intercom, the only obvious way to open the gate. From what I can see, his house is isolated, set back from the street on multiple acres, surrounded by a fucking forest. The only house on the block that's not parading its luxury.

Great.

I place my camera wrap over my head, letting my camera dangle from my chest. I set both my hands on the bars, take a deep breath, and try to jump up. My arms tremble before I let go and I fall less than an inch back to the ground.

Okay, new plan. I look behind me, to my right, and to my left. I follow the brick wall on the left that connects to his gate, walking around to see the rest of the house is not secured. I roll my eyes and walk into the trees. What dummy only puts a gate in the front of his house?

My boots crunch on the fallen leaves as I weave my way through the oak trees. I can see a glimpse of a massive white residence, a few yellow dim lights beaming through the windows, and—

"Fuck!" I trip and catch myself with my hands. I look behind me to see nothing, but beneath my fingers is a coarse, braided texture.

Shit. Shit. Shit.

As soon as I stand, a large net wraps around me. I scream as it launches me into the air and hangs me from a tree. My body is put into a pretzel as I bounce up and down in this trap like a fucking animal.

Well, this is fucking embarrassing.

Chapter Three

Rowan

I stand at the window of my bedroom as I watch the girl fly into the air. A relaxed smile builds on my face as I put my shirt back on. Grabbing my knife from my nightstand, I stride down my stairs, taking two steps at a time.

She really thought she could follow me home. I laugh as I open the front door and walk into my front yard. I can hear her huffing and puffing, trying to get loose. I follow the sounds through the trees.

And then she thinks she can sneak onto my property? Kind of cute how determined she is. Never had a women chase me this hard. I stand a few feet away from her and lean against the oak.

"Hello?" she whispers. "Is someone there?"

I tap my knife against the wood and watch as she struggles to turn around in the net trap.

"Please help me," she begs, her voice sweet and sultry.

"Why were you following me?" I can hear her struggle again but she doesn't respond. "I can keep you here all night, if you wish."

"Oh, fuck off," she seethes.

"Sure thing." I place the knife back in my pocket and stomp my feet through the wilted leaves on the ground without leaving my spot.

"Wait!"

I stop, sucking in the side of my cheek to keep from smiling.

"Wait," she repeats in a whisper. "Please let me down. I'll leave."

"Didn't answer my question."

She sighs, and I envision her face in my head. Her big brown eyes, her heart-shaped face, her pink puckered lips, and her wild curly hair. She was enchanting when she opened the door to the club, her face plastered with all sorts of emotions before she took off running. "What's your name?"

"Celeste."

Celeste, like heaven. Pretty name, for a pretty girl. "Answer the question, Celeste."

"I-I need a photo."

"You're paparazzi?" I lean against the tree again, still looking up at the woman hanging in the air. She can't see me down here and all I can see are her bunched-up legs and arms hanging outside the trap. "Can't be a comfortable position up there," I mock.

"No shit, psycho. Now let me down and I'll leave."

"Oh, but I thought you needed a photo?" I taunt. "Go ahead. Take one."

She's silent so I take out my knife and start carving into the oak, watching the tree bark fall to the ground. I can really be here all night, standing in the freezing air, watching her, listening to her breathe, smelling her scent through the breeze. She smells like honey, with a dash of cinnamon. "How much you make?"

"That's none of your concern."

"Must be a decent amount for a car like yours."

She scoffs. "Says the one driving an Aston Martin. Oh wait, I forgot. Your daddy probably paid for it, huh? Along with this house? All the prostitutes? All the club memberships?"

I tsk. "So, you researched me. Find anything you like?"

She laughs hysterically. "No. Not really."

"Shame. Thought you were here to be one of my prostitutes." I slash the knife through the air, cutting the rope. She screams and lands on the ground.

"What the fuck!" She stands and makes a full three-sixty before finally finding me. "Fucking asshole."

I hum. "I'll make you a deal."

She wipes off the dirt and debris from her pants. "No thanks."

"You can get a photo."

Her hands pause and she looks up, squinting to try and look closer at me.

"I'll make sure it's a good one too."

"Or I can call the cops for this little death trap you have, and holding me hostage," she threatens.

My eyebrows raise. "You're going to call the cops for *you* trespassing?" She looks in the other direction. "Right. So, the deal is, we hang out. That's it. Then you can get the photo."

"Ew. No."

"Ew?" I stop myself from stepping forward into the light.

"Yeah, ew. No thanks, Mr. Harper." She picks up her camera and starts walking away.

I smile as she sways her hips. "See you later, heaven."

She turns around, bunching her nose, and shakes her head. I watch until she is completely off my property, staring in the dark long after she is gone. As soon as I hear her car start from the end of the street, I head back inside.

I walk to my office door, scanning my finger until it unlocks, and pick up my phone to call Jace. I've known Jace for most of my life. He is a pain in my ass, but he is the only person in my life that I trust. He has had my back through thick and thin since we were kids. So making him my business partner was a no-brainer.

I sit at my desk as I wait for him to pick up.

"Ye know Rowan, I don't like being woken up." I ignore him, not caring about his beauty rest and already irritated that he is using his accent. The only time he goes full-blown Irish on me is when he is pissed or wants to piss me off.

"I need you to do research on a girl named Celeste. Paparazzi."

A groan comes from the other end of the line. "This can't wait until the morn—" I hang up the phone before he can finish the sentence.

Celeste

I walk up the stairs to the house and try to pull out my keys. I do my best to open the door as quietly as possible to not wake Lily.

"Oh my god, Celeste! Where have you been?! I have been trying to call you for the past two hours! I almost called the Navy Seals!"

I pull out my phone to see I have twenty missed calls and thirty text messages. "Lily... the Navy Seals would not come looking for me."

Her hands fly into the air. "Well shit, I don't know! What happened to you? It's almost three a.m. and you're aways home before me. Did you get the picture of Rowan? And why are there leaves in your hair?" Lily asks all these questions as she follows me to my room so I can put my camera away and all the way back into the kitchen. I can feel her eyes shooting a hole into the back of my head.

I open the fridge and slam a bottle of wine on the counter, staring at her.

She waves her hands in the air and grabs the bottle, unscrewing it. "No worries. Everything will be fine. It will all work out."

I slide the glass to her and she fills it. "So, what happened?"

"I went to his house."

Lily's eyes open wide and her mouth falls open. "You went to Rowan Harper's house? *The* Rowan Harper?"

"Yeah, he's psycho."

"Like psychologically hot? Or—"

"Gross, Lily."

She grabs my glass and takes a sip. "Oh, absolutely. Rowan's not my type. But he is yours," she sing-songs.

"No, he's not," I repeat in her tone. "I'm tired, dirty, and very much over this conversation, thank you." I snatch the glass back from her and start heading toward my room.

She still follows me. "Fine. I won't ask. No questions here."

I turn around to see her leaning in my doorway. "Did you see his dick? Is it as big as they say?" She waggles her brows and shimmies her shoulders.

"Get out of my room."

I go to close the door, but she stops it with her foot. She inches her head between the door, her full lips puckered, and says, "We will talk about it in the morning, okay, pumpkin?" She blows a kiss and removes her foot so that the door can close.

My forehead hits the wood and I stand there in silence, once again contemplating all my life decisions.

CHAPTER FOUR
CELESTE

I heard Lily leaving the house early this morning. I probably should have told her that last night I was literally stuck in an animal trap. I feel like that is something you should tell your best friend. Maybe not only your best friend, but the whole world? I would probably go viral if I were to make a video and let everyone know that Rowan Harper sets traps along his property for humans. I bet his reputation would go further downhill than it already is.

And it was so weird how he just stayed in the shadows like some ghost. I wanted to get closer and maybe punch or slap him for trapping me, but I saw the knife glistening in his hand and thought otherwise. My life may be a mess, but I'd rather not die before I can clean myself up, make a name for myself.

So, now we are at plan C: painting and selling. I have two days to come up with the cash for Lily even though she said it was no big deal. I want to prove to her and myself that I can do this. "I can do this, right?" I whisper into the blue sky.

"Please give me some strength," I pray. Two girls whisper and stare as they walk past me and I give them an awkward smile before looking down at the camera in my lap.

Central Park is surprisingly quiet today. Or at least the side of the park that I am on. I put my camera to my face and take a picture of the scenery. Two trees are in front of me and the sun shines right through them. Fall is showing in the leaves as they go from bright green to burnt orange, drifting from their branches.

Two men jog by wearing trash bags as sweaters. I quickly snap a picture when their backs are turned. At this point, I will take a picture of anything to get some type of creative juice flowing.

A man walks by, wearing an all-black hoodie with his head down. He sits four benches away from me and never looks up. I keep an eye on him in my peripheral, waiting for him to get on his phone, or get up and walk away, or do something. But he just keeps his head down and his hands intertwined between his knees.

Every time I pick up my camera to take another picture, the hair on the back of my neck rises. I set my camera down and turn to look at him, catching him looking away. Is this weirdo watching me? Lily is good at confrontation. She will call someone out in the middle of the street if they bump into her. But me? I'd apologize for them.

I scan through my photos for the day and feel my heart picking up its pace. I can feel him staring at me. So, listening to my intuition because I am not stupid, I pack my camera back into my bag and begin walking back to the parking garage. As I pass by him, I notice a large gold ring on his finger. I keep my distance and hold my keys in my hand with my keychain pepper spray ready.

I keep peeking over my shoulder—even though nobody is following me. Yet, I can't get this irk-y feeling that I am being followed, like someone is still watching. As soon as I enter the garage, I sprint for my car. I throw the door open and slide into my seat, locking the doors right after. I nearly break my neck looking behind me to make sure the Boogeyman is not in the small crevices of my back seat, waiting for me.

I shrink down into my seat and take a deep breath. "Fucking scaredy cat."

When I get home, I retreat to my bedroom, turn on my music, and grab my art supplies. I toss everything on the bed and stare at my blank canvas, one paint brush in my hand and another in my mouth.

I jump at the sound of the front door slamming, shaking the whole house, followed by a loud squeak of, "Bitch let's go!"

When I look down at my canvas, there is still a big blob of nothingness. I turn to the clock on my bedside table and note that I have been staring at my canvas for over an hour.

My bedroom door is kicked open, Lily standing in the doorway. "Are you not getting my texts?" I look around my sheets covered in paint bottles and brushes, but my phone is nowhere in sight. "I got the night off from the club and I don't have school tomorrow. We are going out."

I groan, falling into my pillows. "Lily, it's three o'clock in the afternoon." And I am nowhere close to creating a painting to sell.

"Okay and? It's five o'clock somewhere. Put on something cute."

"The clubs aren't even open."

"Okay and?! We are going to go somewhere to get alcohol in our systems and then we are going to get into a club when they open and dance our asses off on some hot dudes until we cannot feel our feet. Now hurry up and get your cute ass off the bed and get dressed!"

Lily is out of the doorframe before I can even protest. It wouldn't matter anyway. Nobody can say no to her.

I drag my body off the bed, jump in the shower, quickly do my hair and makeup, and put on an outfit.

Lily comes into my room with a toothbrush dangling from her mouth. "Oh no, no, no." As she shakes her head, toothpaste falls from her mouth, forcing her to slurp the contents. "You're not wearing that." She points up and down at my outfit.

"What's wrong with this?" I look down at my black crop top, ripped jeans, and Doc Martens.

"I said hot dudes in the club. Not a parent-teacher conference." She opens my closet door and starts throwing my clothes off the hangers. I stand there waiting, leaning on my dresser with my hands crossed over my chest.

Half of my closet lays across the floor, with Lily complaining every third shirt that I need more color in my life. She turns around, holding up a lacy bustier camisole she bought for me two years ago that I have yet to wear.

"Jeans. This shirt. Heels." She holds the top to my chest.

"What is this? 2014?"

"Your double Ds in this..." She puts her fingers to her mouth and kisses them like a chef.

"Should I search for my bangles and my six-inch stilettos?"

Her eyes go wide. "Ohmygod, yes!"

I roll my eyes and snatch the shirt from her hand. I squeeze my breasts into the camisole and turn to face the mirror, seeing my balloons ready to choke me to death.

"Taxi's here. Shoes now," Lily states, staring at her phone and leaving my room.

Why do I ever take her advice? No idea. But she's never been wrong when it comes to fashion. My tits do look good, and my waist is snatched. But I defer on the bangles and stilettos. I quickly slide my feet into some small wedges when Lily starts yelling from the living room. I snatch my handbag from my dresser and run out of the house with Lily.

"Can you tell me about Rowan now? What does he smell like up close? Did you at least touch his abs? Are they real or are they fake? I saw recently some music artist got his abs done and it looks ridiculous."

I turn fully to Lily and side-eye the taxi driver who keeps looking in the rearview mirror. "I went to his house."

"Yes, we have established that. I want more! Did you see his dick or not?!"

"No, Lil. I couldn't even see his face." I can feel the driver still eye-fucking us through his mirror. He seems familiar. Like someone I've felt before—presence-wise. But it's also extremely hard to tell when you see over a thousand faces a day walking through the city.

"You're a little liar. I know you're hiding something from me." Lily puts down her lipstick and mirror she was using and scoots closer to the partition in the taxi. "Keep your eyes on the road, you fucking perv." She points her red Marilyn Monroe-inspired lipstick at me. "Liar, liar, pants on fire."

"Let's just get drunk so I can forget about it."

"That, I can do for you."

Six hours and an unknown amount of drinks later, both of us are giggling down the street to our next destination. My feet are blistered for sure, but my body is completely numb. Our next club has a line that wraps around the whole building.

"Lily, I have to pee again." I jump up and down and squeeze her arm.

"I got this." She ignores the line behind the red rope and heads straight to the bouncer. "Hey, Josh," she intones. The bouncer turns around and smiles at her. She puts her hand on his shoulder and stands on her tippy toes, leaning into his ear. When she retreats, he looks her up and down and looks behind her at me before giving her a nod. He stands to the side and lets us through the door. Lily rubs her hand down his arm as we walk by and turns to me with a wink as she pulls us inside.

"What did you say to him?"

"I told him to meet me in the bathroom." She drags us through the crowd and pushes her way into the bathroom with, thankfully, no line. I run like hell into the stall and squat to let the waterfall of alcohol stream out of me.

After what feels like an eternity of holding my arms on the graffiti stall walls and squatting above the disgusting toilet while my legs shake with fear, I walk out of the stall at the same time the bouncer walks in.

"Oh, wow. You guys are serious?" I look at Lily through the bathroom mirror, washing my hands.

She giggles, shrugging her shoulders. "Go get us drinks. This should be quick."

I laugh and clasp my hands on the bouncer's chest on my way out. "Go easy—"

"Oh, I won't," the bouncer says.

I snort and nod my head to my best friend who is leaning against the bathroom sink. "I was talking to her."

I can see the bouncer's Adam's apple bob as he takes a hesitant step further into the bathroom.

This club is darker than most, almost like Club Opal. The black flashing lights make it look more like a haunted house than a dance club. Every step I take feels like I didn't move from my original spot. Pushing through everyone dancing around me, I head to the bartender and order us two vodka crans. I turn around and wait for the bartender to make my potential hangover drink and survey the crowd around me. The dance floor is packed with people swaying to the music. Even with sweat building at the nape of my neck, I get this icy chill followed by goosebumps rising against my arms. My heart syncs with the bass of the music and I get a sudden rush of anxiety.

I turn to check on the drinks, but the bartender is still focused on some fancy cocktail. I look at the people around me. They're all in their own worlds being their own main characters, yet my anxiety is still ricocheting off my body. My head becomes light, dizzy—

"Wow, I needed that." Lily smooths down her hair, wipes the smeared mascara from underneath her eyes, and pats her flushed cheeks.

My heart slows and I take a large inhale. "Condom?"

"What am I? A noob? Of course I used a condom." She reaches behind me and hands me our drinks. "Can you imagine?" She laughs. "Me? A mother?!" She grabs my arm and escorts us to the dance floor.

My drink slides down the side of my lips as I take one huge gulp. Lily parks us in the middle of the pit. Her body waves against mine and I follow suit. We seductively move in unison, our hips as one with the beat, one hand in the air holding our drinks and the other hand exploring each other's bodies.

Lily's swaying slows as her eyes move above my head and widen. She takes a step back and grins before turning around to grab a random guy behind her to dance on. I look to my right and my left, checking for my next dance partner. Before I can roam around, hands lock on my hips, pressing hard to hold my back against them.

Ice flows down my spine and settles deep in the pit of my stomach. I try to turn around, but these hands hold me in place. I press further back against him, and he has the audacity to push me an inch away. I reach my hands in the air to try and grab or hold onto something, but the closet thing I can reach are his shoulders.

Okay, this is weird? Are we going to stand here while he has a death grip on my hips the whole time? Does he not know how to dance? I try once more to squirm from his hold, twisting my hips until his arm wraps around my stomach and slams me back into his chest. His face is shoved into my neck, and I can feel his lips against my skin. He smells like mint and leather, and his breath sends electricity down to my toes.

My knees beg to buckle when his tongue darts out and licks the salt from my skin. He removes the hold he has on me as the song ends. I stumble over my feet hurriedly to turn around, but by then, his back is facing me as he pushes through the crowd. He floats away with the flashing lights, and my first thought is to chase this stranger. I need a name, number, or fuck, an address. I mean, who licks someone and then scurries off like nothing happened?

As soon as I take a step in his direction, Lily steps in front of me, her hands landing on my shoulders and her face a pale green to match her eyes. Her cheeks widen like a blowfish, and I grab her arm to run her out of the crowd.

☆ Chapter Five
Celeste

Pounding. Sweet Jesus, my eyes are pounding. I crack one open and see my clock blinking 7 a.m. I am a wet, soggy, overcooked noodle that has been thrown in the garbage disposal, and I wish for nothing more than a large cup of coffee and a bottle of the strongest ibuprofen.

I roll onto my back and stare at the ceiling. One too many drinks and I start hallucinating little fairies giggling above me—wait, no. I roll to my side again and envision my ears widening.

That's Lily's giggle. I thought when we left the club, she was a shot away from alcohol poisoning. How the hell did she manage to bring a guy home? I pull the covers above my head to try and fall back asleep, but her giggles are louder and the guy's voice is familiar.

I swing my legs from the bed, feeling the cold floor beneath my feet. If it's the bouncer, I swear I will hang this over her head for the rest of her life. *"My best friend fell in love the day she*

*fucked her husband in the bar bathroom because I
needed to pee."*

I walk into the kitchen and open the fridge
to grab a water bottle. When I turn around, I see two
faces staring at me. My eyes are still trying to adjust
to the curtains being open, letting in the bright,
soul-sucking sunlight.

I see Lily, sitting on the couch, still in the
same clothes from last night. I take two long blinks
and squint my eyes. The other face is Rowan
Harper.

I choke on my water from the sharp inhale,
turning to the sink to cough as the liquid flows
through my nose. I'm choking so hard I fear I might
throw up, and I swear if it happens in my kitchen
sink right here, right now, in front of Rowan, I am
going to end my life.

When I catch my breath, I turn back around
to see a smirk on Rowan's face. "Good morning."
He is holding two plastic coffee cups, and my feet
drag me straight in front of him. I wipe my nose
with my arm and snatch a cup away from him.

I look at Lily, who's cuddled up on the
couch. She wiggles her eyebrows but then points
behind Rowan's back and points inside her mouth,
pretending to gag.

"Get dressed."

"Huh?" I look back at Rowan. His chiseled
jaw clenches and I look down at my large

SpongeBob shirt that barely stops at my crotch. I grab the hem and tug it down. "What the fuck are you doing here?" I look back at Lily. "Why the fuck is he here?!"

"Potty mouth."

"Stalker?!" I take a sip of the coffee in my hands and thank the heavens that it's iced and caramel. This is my first time I am inches away from Rowan, *the* Rowan Harper, the billionaire bachelor, the "I date any women who has a hole between her thighs and a mouth that can work" Rowan Harper. The. Rowan. Harper. And nobody has ever noticed or brought up that he has a large scar that starts at his ear and cuts into the middle of his cheek. Yet, it has no impact on his annoyingly handsome look.

He leans in close to me. "I would like to presume you stalked me first."

"Well, you persumed wrong."

"Presumed."

"Don't correct me in my own house." My head is spinning, and I'd like to sit down now.

His lip twitches. "Go get dressed, Celeste."

I lean to the side to look around his tall, wide pack of muscles that shouldn't exists in a businessman body. "Um, help?"

Lily kicks her feet up on the coffee table. "Eh, I kind of want to see how this pans out."

Rowan uses his fingers to turn my chin back to him. "Today will be worth it, Celeste. Just go get dressed."

I stare into his rich brown eyes, mapping certain beauty marks splattered on his face. His dark black waves shadow his forehead. His nose has a prominent bridge with a slight bend. I can see why women fall for him. He looks like he belongs on one of those Italian soap operas. The ones like *Romeo and Juliet*, minus the age gap, minus the death. Just lots of love triangles and cheating. I bet someone would write a book about him and use him as inspiration.

"Pass." I walk away, into my hallway, and into my room. I use my foot to close the door behind me, but it bounces back, hitting my wall. I turn around to find him leaning against the doorframe.

"Why are you being so hardheaded?"

"Hardheaded? Am I a child?! And you almost put a hole in the wall! Stop screaming at me!"

He chuckles. "You're the one screaming." He wraps his arms around his chest, showing off the biceps that could tear his shirt if he flexes any harder. "Just like a child. If I had to assume, what are you? Twenty-one? Twenty-two?"

"Twenty-four. What are you? Eighty-seven? Eighty-six?"

"Ouch."

"I'm not a prostitute, Mr. Harper. Go find someone else." I wave my hand at him.

"I didn't know showing up to someone's house, offering them coffee and a fun day meant assuming they were a sex worker?" He raises an eyebrow at me and I deflate into my skin.

I have nothing against sex workers. I am all for it. Shit, the club Lily works at offers sex. But what I'd rather not do is be caught with him in public and have my face plastered all over the magazines as his new girlfriend. "You're not going to give up, are you?" I sigh.

He shakes his head.

"Don't you have a girlfriend?"

"No," he states.

"And I am supposed to trust you?"

"Yes."

I pinch my eyes, contemplating if he is lying. I am oddly exceptional at calling out a liar. When I don't see any signs or feel any tingles down my spine, I sigh, to truly let him know that I am not ecstatic about this. That I'd rather treat my hungover body in a comfy bed. In the comfort of my own home. I reach for the door, ready to close it. "Get out so I can change."

CHAPTER SIX
ROWAN

Thanks to Jace, I was able to ruin my heaven's morning. It took ten minutes for him to send me all the information he found on Celeste. She's an orphan from Chatham, Massachusetts. Saved up enough money to move to Brooklyn. Never had a home address until she met Lily. She's been in the paparazzi business since she was eighteen—but fuck the paparazzi, this woman can paint. Vibrant, odd, expressive paintings that are extremely unconventional. Paintings that I soon will be adding to my collection.

I was easily able to trace her phone last night to find her running around New York. I couldn't help but follow her, wondering what she was doing. Was she working? Was she going for a midnight snack? A jog? Why was she going to so many different clubs? Was she running away from someone who was trying to kidnap her?

Of course, my brain imagined the worst. So I jumped onto my bike, left Club Opal, and headed to her location. As soon as I saw her on the dance floor with Lily, I had to intervene. I wanted her to stop dancing, stop dancing for everyone to see. And wanted her to keep dancing, but only for me. When the song was over, I left her. If I had stayed, everything would have escalated, and that's not how I want things to go. She obviously believes what she sees in the paper and online—I can't completely blame her. But now I have to prove to her that I don't stick my dick between every pair of legs I see.

From the conversation I had with Lily, she either couldn't see me last night because of how drunk she was or because the club was too dark. Either way, my little mishap—not being able to keep myself away from her—was not caught.

As soon as we get into my car, she faces the passenger side window. I can see the tension and apprehensiveness all over her face. Her emotions worn plainly like a mask. I turn the music up to try and help with the silence, not knowing how to make conversation with a girl I practically guilted into hanging out with me. I haven't done this in years, never really needed to. Girls don't want dates. They want my dick and sometimes I'm happy to oblige. But something about Celeste from the first day I caught her in my yard made me want to... Shit, I don't know? Slow down? She is infatuating, her beauty and sharp tongue. I only want to know her more.

"Where are we going? And can you tell me how you found out where I lived now?" Irritation streams through every word. I keep my eyes forward, focusing on traffic with one hand gripping the steering wheel.

"Do you like your job?"

"No, don't change the subject. If I am being kidnapped to be slaughtered, I'd like to know now."

"Have to delete your search history?"

Her eyebrows pinch together. "Do you like your daddy paying for everything?"

"Do you like people assuming your dick is small from the car you drive?" I swivel my head back and forth from the road to her. Her mouth opens, ready to catch a fly.

"*Do you like people assuming your dick is small from the car you drive*?!" she repeats, extremely fast.

"I have witnesses who can attest otherwise." I wink at her, and her lip curls before huffing and looking back out the window.

I laugh, stepping on the gas to get us through this traffic.

I put my car in park when we reach our destination. On my left, John is already parked and waiting for me to get out of the car. Celeste looks out the window to notice there are only trees, bushes, and one rocky path up a mountain.

"I am going to assume I am not dying today since your dickhead military officer tagged along."

"Very meticulous of you." I exit the vehicle and John hands me a camera bag. I turn around and give it to Celeste. She tilts her head to the side and stares at the bag in confusion. "If you're going to take photos of me, it's going to be with a high-quality camera."

"There's nothing wrong with my camera."

Her camera was made in the early 2000s and maybe takes photos fine, but I think she deserves better. And if there is going to be a photo of me, a full photo—an actual photo that I am going to pose for—it's going to be in high resolution.

I watch as she opens the bag and pulls the camera out. Her face morphs from shock to confusion, to... anger?

"You're joking. This is a Leica SL2. I can't take this!" She holds it out to me as if it's going to give her some type of disease. And since I'm not taking no for an answer, I walk away, heading toward the trail. I can hear her footsteps stomping behind me as we walk up the dirt path and into an overgrown section.

"Mr. Harper!"

I push my way through the shrubbery, getting off the main trail to avoid people. Celeste continues to call my name with a heavy breath. I hear a couple of curse words along with a tree branch crunching. I continue to follow my memory of the land until I hear the creek flowing.

"Is this, right here, okay?" I turn around to see Celeste bent over, hands on her knees. "You have asthma or something?"

"Or something." She stands and takes a deep inhale. "What are we doing?"

"You needed a photo."

She looks down at the camera in her hand and the lightbulb flickers above her head. "Are you serious?"

"If I wasn't, I don't think we would be here, Miss Jones." She rolls her eyes, something she is incredibly good at. "Can we hurry this along?"

"Don't rush me," she mumbles, flicking at the buttons on the camera, then holds it to her face. "There is no full photo of your face anywhere."

I don't respond. I stand between two trees as still as a statue. This photo is going to be ridiculous. I can already see the tabloids: *Rowan Harper caught lost in the woods. Rowan Harper damaged his face while high on LSD and wandering New York's forest. Is Rowan Harper being sent to rehab, again?*

"Is it because of the scar?" she questions.

"I believe it's rude to meddle in someone's business."

The camera falls from her face. "I think it's rude to stalk and kidnap but you don't hear me complaining."

"Actually, you *did* complain." I turn around to head further into the forest. Celeste calls out for me again with her thick boots stomping behind me. I stop when we reach the ledge and stare at the pool, digging my heels into the ground when Celeste runs into me from behind.

"Shi— Woah." Her eyes widen, staring at the waterfall and looking over the edge down to the pool. "What is this place?"

"A... waterfall." She snaps to me and squints her eyes. I used to come here with my mother as a kid when my father, Lance, was having a "bad day," as my mother would tell me.

My mother was a paranoid woman, so we would avoid the main trails and ended up finding this waterfall. I used to get so excited coming here, jumping into the water with her, feeling the ice-cold pool wash away all the pain and worries as a kid. I guess I never got rid of the routine. I continue to come here when I need it. Sometimes I sit on the ledge and watch the sun gleam from the water. Sometimes I jump in to wash away the anger. Sometimes I just come to think.

I start to remove my clothes, kicking off my shoes and ripping my shirt over my head.

"What are you—"

I cut her off by jumping over the ledge. The water silences everything. I force myself to stay under, eyes closed, lungs burning. When I push myself up, I shake out my hair and wipe the droplets from my eyes. I look up to see Celeste on her hands and knees, gripping the edge of the drop. "Are you insane?!" She yells loud enough that the birds flee from the branches.

I wave my hand, suggesting she join me. She stares down at me for a while, her expression stuck on one emotion: fear. "I promise it's safe."

"I'm supposed to trust you?!"

"Yes."

She contemplates for a second longer before finally getting up. She slowly removes her shirt and snatches off her boots. Her pants. She disappears from my vision before her high-pitched scream is heard, and her tiny legs splay in the air. Before she hits the water, she turns into a pencil. Her head immediately bobs to the surface, "Ohfuckme, this is freezing!" Her teeth chatter as she slicks her curly black hair out of her face and her eye makeup smudges like a raccoon. "This is so pretty," she says, staring at the fall above us.

"Yes."

She looks back at me and scrunches her nose before she disappears beneath the waves. I follow her until we are underneath the waterfall. She picks herself up and onto the ledge and holds her hands out to feel the falling water. I decide to stay beneath, hiding the unbelievable growing urge in my boxers. Can't tell you why I thought this would be a fun or good idea. She is practically naked. She's not in a thong or anything, nothing lacy or stringy. Yet her undergarments are still revealing. Short underwear that has half her ass hanging out and her boobs are— I look away, turning my back on her and raising my elbows to rest on the ledge.

"This was fun," she says.

I keep my eyes in the distance and hum my acknowledgment to her. Her hand claps on my shoulder and my body tenses. "But, time to go home, Mr. Harper."

I snark and continue to kick my feet in the water.

"Fine." She stands up and squeezes the water from her hair. "I'll go ask your military, bodyguard, weirdo to take me home."

"His name is John."

"Yeah, whatever." She walks away, following the path behind the fall that leads to up a hill. "Nice knowing you, Mr. Harper. Thanks for allowing me to take a photo so I can keep my job, and you can continue to be famous." She gives me the middle finger without turning around. I watch and watch until she hits the hill, looking up at it to see how high up she has to climb. She shakes out her hand and tries to grasp into the muddy wall, lifts one foot, and slides right back down.

She tries two more times before finally giving up and turning around. "How the hell do we get out of here?!"

I bite my tongue, holding in a laugh, and get out of the water. I walk in the opposite direction where there are stone steps to bring us back up the hill and to our clothes. Once we're dressed, we walk silently side by side until we are back in the parking lot. John is sitting in his car with his seat leaning all the way back and Celeste walks to the passenger door—

"What the fuck do you think you're doing?"

Celeste looks over her shoulder. "I'm not going with you."

"Yes. You are."

"Oh, so now I am being stalked, kidnapped, and held hostage?"

"I believe being held hostage and kidnapped are in the same category."

She snorts and opens the door. John lifts his chair upright and starts the car. Before she can slide into the seat, I grab her hips and throw her over my shoulder. She screams and kicks at my back and thankfully there is no one in this parking lot.

Another night in jail will really put the nail in the coffin for my investors.

"Let go of me!"

I kick the car door shut and knock on the roof of John's car. Walking around mine while Celeste screams bloody murder, I throw her in the vehicle and slam her door shut. I watch her through the window as I march around the front of the car to make sure she doesn't take off. Her eyes follow mine with her arms crossed against her chest.

"Not cool, dude," she says when I sit in the car. "I hope someone saw us so that tomorrow morning when you wake up, you see your face plastered all over the news and the cops bang down your pretty little house and put you in handcuffs. What will it be? Your fifth strike? What is that, like life in prison now?"

"Do you believe everything you read on the internet?" I back out of the dirt parking lot and take us back to the main road.

"Do you stalk and kidnap every girl you first meet?"

"You're not using those terms very lightly, Miss Jones."

"I never told you my last name!" She huffs and squirms in the seat. "You know what, it doesn't matter. I shouldn't be surprised that you know my last name. But since you're such a know-it-all about

Celeste Jones, riddle me this, Mr. Harper, what is my blood type?"

"B negative."

"Ha! Trick question. I don't even know my blood type." She lifts her chin like she's proving something to herself.

"Wild guess," I tell her. Except it's not a wild guess. That is her blood type. On March 7, 2023, she was in the hospital for stomach pain and excessive bleeding on her cycle. She was diagnosed with polycystic ovary syndrome. They kept her in the hospital overnight and released her. Told her there was nothing she could do except get on birth control.

I've never heard of that diagnosis before, so I did my own research. Fucking unbelievable how little scientists and doctors care for the female anatomy. Polycystic ovary syndrome has so many links to other things like endometriosis. After reading the symptoms, I realized endometriosis is like cancer. It fucking grows and strangles your organs to death. Your own damn tissue, just growing outside the uterus like a damn cancerous vine. And polycystic ovary syndrome, tumors. That's what they are. Or like a second-degree burn, just blistering on the ovaries that can pop and leak, and extremely painful. I read a blog where a woman talking about her symptoms said they are worse than childbirth. Yet there is no actual cure for either of them.

I glance at Celeste in my peripheral. She sits in the seat staring out the passenger window. Her arms are still crossed. When I read over her medical records, I immediately wanted to burst into her room at five in the morning and hold her. Instead, she sits in the passenger seat of my car having an attitude because I am taking her home at her request—sort of. Either way, sorry Celeste Jones, but it's going to be hard getting rid of me so easily. I have so much I still would like to explore.

Chapter Seven
Celeste

I text Lily to ask when she has another night off. I
have more memories I would like to forget with a
cheap, disgusting drink that will probably taste like
toilet bowl water that includes an unholy amount of
liquor that should not be ingested within a span of
two minutes. And I need it to happen soon.

I take a peek at the man at my side who sits
comfortably in his luxury car even though his
substantial height forces his head to touch the roof
of the vehicle and—cheese on a stick, has anyone
seen a man drive? Are we okay as women? I know I
am not the only one who gets turned on by the way
a man drives. The leaned-back posture, one hand on
the steering wheel, veins protruding from the
forearm down to the hands…

I roll my eyes. Gather yourself, Celeste. I
am extremely proud of myself for not making a fuss
when he took off his clothes and showed off his
intricate tattoos and muscles. And muscles on top of
muscles. Of muscles on muscles. Can't let Mr.
Rowan Harper's head get any bigger than it already

is. "I'll download the photos onto my computer, and you can have your camera back."

"Keep it," he says groggily.

You know what? I will keep it. He has enough money in his daddy's bank account to buy another or two. I, on the other hand, will be back into negatives once I sell this photo and pay rent.

"Hungry?" he asks.

"Nope."

I grab on to the door handle when he cuts across traffic into a small diner in the middle of nowhere.

"Well, I am." He turns off his car and exits the vehicle. I slam my head back against the headrest and send a silent prayer to whoever is listening that this diner catches on fire as soon as we walk in. The passenger door opens, and Rowan waits for me to exit.

We walk in and are told to take a seat anywhere we like. I follow Rowan to a booth and quickly scan the menu. Cheeseburger, bacon cheeseburger, fish and chips, tacos, sushi, gyros... My lip curls in disgust. When a diner has a multi-cuisine menu, I immediately assume I will be receiving food poisoning. I can't explain the reasoning for it, I just assume.

Military dick—John—enters the establishment and sits two rows behind us. "Are you even friends with him?"

"Who?"

I nod to who just took a seat behind him and he shrugs his shoulders. "He's my employee."

The waitress quickly takes our order and says it will be right up. I send another silent prayer that my burger is not dropped on the floor and put back on the grill to "burn off any germs." Rowan intertwines his fingers on the table and stares at me.

I mimic him and say, "So."

"So."

"How 'bout that Rowan Empire?"

He quietly snorts, trying to hide it with his chin tucked into his shoulder.

"Or that crypto. Really boomin', huh?"

He bites the inside of his cheek. "Yeah, I believe with JA Mining, the rise of meme coins will soon become a US regulation and outweigh the current spot ETFs."

My face flattens. "Ew."

He smirks and looks out the window. "Everyone believes I work for my father at his real estate company. Well, I do work for my father, but I have my own private investigation company."

"Fascinating," I snark. "I forgot that you can add 'stalking people for a living' in your resume."

"Oh, I'm sorry, Miss Jones." He cocks his head to the side. "Please remind me what you do for a living again?" He leans back against the booth, crossing his arms, which causes his shirt to tighten against his chest, his pecs outlined by the thin fabric. I straighten my posture and clear my throat. We have a stare off for the next few minutes, my eye twitching with irritation as I struggle to not lose all self-control by fixating on the bulging biceps, or the protruding chest, or the face that is handsome enough to be put into a museum.

I jump in my seat when my phone vibrates the table. I quickly pick it up to see Lily's message.

Lil: When you suck his dick, make sure to record. Imagine all the money you'll make online.

My eyes could be seen rolling to the back of my head, and I place my phone screen down back on the table.

When the food arrives, I'm no longer hungry. Both Rowan and I stare at the unappetizing platters placed in front of us. I think I can see the E. Coli floating around in the lettuce and ohmygod, is that a hair?!

"Um," Rowan says, pushing his eyebrows together as he stares at what I also believe to be a burger on the plate. He leans forward toward me. "I think—"

"You know, for our first date, I expected a lunch or dinner at more of an elegant place, or—"

"Date?"

I look up at him, my eyes widening. "No— I mean…"

He laughs, slamming a hundred-dollar bill on the table before standing and practically running out of the diner. I follow him with his bodyguard on my tail. I jump into his car and before I can put my seatbelt on, he takes off speeding, forcing my head to slam back on the headrest. "Don't actually kill me now!"

He grins at me and changes gears to go even faster.

When we make it to my house, I quickly get out the car. Bending down through the window, I tell him, "Nice knowing you, for real now. Please don't ever contact me again."

He grins, giving me the most mischievous eyes. "Yep, see you later, heaven."

"No—" I fall back when he takes off, cutting a car off and speeding through the intersection in front of my house. "Fucking shit."

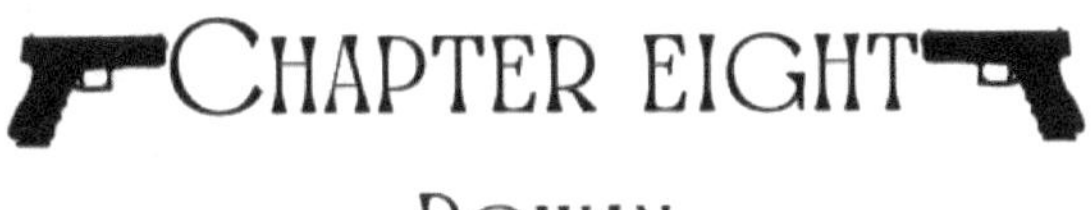CHAPTER EIGHT

ROWAN

I smile as I swerve through traffic, nodding my head to the music playing through my car speakers. I haven't felt this *light* in a while. As if I have no worries in the world. I've been going to the fall for months now, chasing this feeling, but when I duck my head beneath the water, I've come up feeling ten times heavier. But today, today was nice. I might have to blame it on the five-foot-nothing brat that I forced to come with me.

She's funny and has a smart mouth. I think I'll keep her around for a while. She believes everything that is written about me. The sex, party, drugs, alcohol—whatever else is being told in the magazines, and I don't blame her. I usually give no fucks about what people think of me, but with Celeste Jones, I'll prove to her that I am more than what society portrays me to be.

I pull to the curb of Club Opal, already late for the night. Thankfully it's not busy and I don't have to hide from the paparazzi. I pull back the red curtains of our VIP section to see Jace already working. "You're late," he says without lifting his head from the computer.

"Any leads?"

It's been three years, and they still haven't found my mother. It took them five months to give up. Five months for them to assume she is dead. But I refuse. I refuse to believe that the woman who gave me life just upped and disappeared from her home. I will find her. My father has always been a prick, but since my mother—Joan Harper—went missing, he has been even more impassive. Lance Harper, the big CEO of Harper International, refused to let the world know his own wife was missing. No new reports. No newspaper article.

He said it would be bad for business.

Yet he allows all the lies the magazine articles say about *me*.

I slam my breaks once I reach the tip of the driveway, jumping out of my car without turning off the engine or closing my door. I walk up to the officer who stands near Lance. There are six other cops exiting the house and search dogs barking in the distance in the cold dark night. "I'm sorry this has happened, Rowan and Mr. Harper, but we will find her." The officer nods once at my father before walking away.

"A deposit was transferred out of Harper International for 1.5 million dollars a week before Joan went missing. And another 2.3 million three weeks after," Jace states, snapping me out of my memories.

"Who does it go to?" I lean over to see the transactions on the laptop. Why would that much money be transferred so close to the time of my mom's disappearance? My hands clench in my lap and my jaw ticks with every scroll on the screen.

"I'm sorry, but I can't get past the wall to see where it goes." Jace slams his back onto the couch. I continue staring at the screen. I had confronted Lance once about the business and the shit he does. He made me the COO when I turned seventeen, but he immediately blocked me from dealing with any of the finances and never informs me of the meetings.

I never wanted to work for him, let alone *with* him.

"Why the fuck was there a meeting without my knowledge, Lance?" I snap.

"There are certain things you just don't need to know," he says, leaning further back in his Rockefeller leather chair.

I put my hands on his desk, my nails scratching into the glass. I'm so close to his face that I can smell the whiskey on his breath. "You shouldn't be CEO anymore if you are obviously having memory issues. You're the one who made me your COO, and if I remember correctly a COO has the right to be in a meeting."

Lance stands from his chair, buttoning his onyx suit, and cracks his neck to each side. I stand at my full height, forcing him to look up at me. I catch his hand sneaking into his suit pocket and bring out his switchblade. I scoff, backing away and leaning onto his ceiling-to-floor office window. He stalks toward me, standing toe to toe, and I clench my jaw to hide the tremble.

Lance has always been quicker than me. Catching me before I could run. That's why when the blade flashes in front of my eyes with a ruby color, I bring my fingers to the side of my cheek and jerk my hand back when the cut stings.

"Threaten me and my job again, and it will be your throat next."

The scar on my face tingles from the memory. He's always had anger issues. Any time he and my mother fought, instead of laying hands on her, he would come to me. My mother would scream in the background, begging him to stop.

I was eight when he broke my nose, ten when he gave me a black eye, twelve when he split my cheek open. But I would rather take the hits than watch my mother be abused, so at some point in my life, I became numb. I began to expect it and accept it.

I was barely nineteen when I came home with my cheek sliced open after work. My mother took one look at me and ran to her room.

Biggest Fan

Now that I'm older, twice his size, faster, and smarter, the physical abuse has stopped. Instead, he's found other avenues to try and destroy me.

Rowan Harper Indulges in a Public Threesome. Rowan Harper, COO of Harper International, Partakes in Drugs, Incarcerated. The list goes on and on. None of it is true. I know my reputation is being tainted to prove to the committee that I'm not worthy of the CEO title. Which I don't want in the first place, but what I do want is to destroy my father.

Lily steps into our VIP room with a bottle of Macallan. Jace perks up. "Good evening, Miss *álainn.*" I don't understand what *álainn* means, and I don't know why he calls Lily that every time he sees her, but I do know that it irritates her.

She is Club Opal's top entertainer. She smiles at everyone, laughs at all the corny jokes, and gives extra attention to the men with money. The only person she refuses to pay attention to is Jace.

"It's Lily," she snaps, giving him a cold stare, which causes Jace to fall back into his seat. She pours the drink into my glass and brings her emerald eyes to mine, mentally shooting daggers at me. "Whatever the fuck you did to Celeste, cut it out. I revoke any invitations I may have given you when I was still drunk."

"Aw man, how am I supposed to tell the wedding planner we need to cancel with such short notice?" I say wryly.

She scoffs, straightening her mini skirt, her lip twitching before she turns on her heels and walks out of the room.

"What the fuck was that about?" Jace says, burning a hole in the side of my face. I grab my glass and shoot it down my throat, feeling the burn make its way to the pit of my stomach.

"Focus on what I pay you to do." I reach for my phone in my pocket and pull up the app I recently installed. I can see Celeste on her bed watching TV. A few seconds later, she reaches down under the covers, her head falling back with lust written on her face. I close the app and open my messages.

Me: Miss me already?

I open the app again to see she has jumped out of bed and is staring at her phone. I go back to our messages, watching the three little dots appear and disappear.

Celeste: Who is this?

Me: Should I come over and fix this need of yours?

The guy I hired installed three cameras in her room and two in her living room. And I may have also had him make a copy of her key. I watch as she throws her phone on the bed and runs out of the room.

Me: Is that a no?

Message Undeliverable

"Son of a bitch." I snatch the laptop away from Jace.

"What the feck, man?!"

I type away, opening a new tab on our program, and infiltrate her Wi-Fi. I run the codes until her password clears and I'm able to hack into her phone through her own network. I go through her block list and un-block myself. Satisfied, with a grin, I hand Jace his laptop back and send a new message.

Me: Don't do that again.

CHAPTER NINE
CELESTE

I stare at the new message on my phone from the same number I just blocked. I swear I just blocked it. Was there a glitch? Did I not do it correctly? Also, the "should I come over and fix this *need* of yours," message was absolutely terrifying. I slowly set my phone back down on the bed and gaze over into the corners of my room.

I'm being paranoid. It was probably some weird advertising or one of those prank texts. But that paranoia did turn me off, so I throw my laptop on the bed and press the block button. *Again.* I swear these text messages are getting worse. The other day I received a text message of an obvious scam saying my package couldn't be delivered... It was a group chat with twenty other numbers. Like, c'mon, how dumb do they think we are? I did get a chuckle out of it when someone responded saying "fuck off."

I open my laptop, plug in the camera, and lean back as the photos start to upload.

"Paycheck, paycheck, paycheck," I silently chant. Once they finish, I lean forward and start scrolling. "Woah." Maybe Rowan was right, I did need a new camera. The quality of some of these are amazing. I wouldn't have to color-grade any of these.

The lighting, the angles—and Rowan doesn't look like he does in all the other photos that are plastered all over social media or magazines. In these photos he looks actually... happy? He's even facing forward and showing off his scar, a scar that no paparazzi has been able to catch and no media outlet has talked about.

I pull up Google and search Rowan Harper, hitting images just to be sure.

In every photo, he somehow angles his face to one side, like a professional. So why did he let me take these full-frame photos? I let out a heavy sigh, pulling the pictures back up. This feels wrong. If he doesn't want his face shown, why show it to me?

I slam the computer shut, throwing it to the side at the edge of my bed. "Mother fucker." I rub at my eyes while I contemplate my whole existence. Why do I have to have feelings? Why can't I just be numb like the rest of this dog-eat-dog world. Any other person would sell these photos in a heartbeat and cash out that check like their life depended on it.

"Ahhh!" I let out a frustrated scream, kicking my feet and bunching my hands on the mattress. I sit up from my bed, rubbing the palms of my hands through my hair, and take a calm, deep breath. Bending down under the bed, I pull out my box of art supplies.

I walk into the post office with my paintings packaged and a huge fucking grin on my face. I practically skipped here—no, I ran here when I woke up this morning and saw the balance on my website account. I did a few paintings last night, not having any thought or care if they sold or not.

And thank the fucking heavens they sold. Because that means I don't have to sell the photos of Rowan, which means he can't come and threaten me again because I owe him for showing his whole face or something. I don't know, I came up with a million and one excuses last night on why I shouldn't do it.

And now I don't have to.

I click my heels together, waiting for the worker to print my receipt. The person who bought the paintings offered over three times the amount. I do get curious about who buys my art. I assume every artist does. I would love to walk into their house and see where they decide to hang it, what they pair it with. I look at the label again printed on the box. My art is being sent to a PO Box located here in the city, but the chances of running into them are close to zero.

After leaving the post office, I head down to Lily's job. She spots me as soon as my boots touch the tile floor. She reaches somewhere behind her and holds out my coffee. Everyone standing in line gives me an ugly stare down, but I take my coffee, raising it to them in a salute with a thin smile, and take the seat next to the table by the window.

I pull my laptop from my bag and open all my media tabs. The first blog that pops up is regarding Rowan and his father, Lance Harper. CEO of Harper International.

Harper International, one of the biggest companies in New York Estes, falls below their market this morning.

I start to read the article, my eyebrows pinching at every big stock market word. If this article is true, maybe that's why he was eager to let me sell the photos. He and his family are running out of money? Business failing and needed some more commotion?

"If you're curious, you can ask."

I squeeze my chair's armrest, turning around to see Rowan standing behind me. He's wearing an all-black suit outlining every muscle. Two buttons are undone at his neckline, showing off the tattoos scattered across his neck: two dragons that face each other as if they are in battle. Their bodies swirl around his neck and down to the start of his chest.

I slam my laptop shut, unable to take my eyes off him. He raises a brow with a smile playing on his lip. "Good to see you, Miss Jones."

"I said I didn't want to see you again."

He nods his head. "Can a man get some coffee?" He points at Lily, who stands behind the register with her middle finger raised toward him. I didn't tell her much the other day when he dropped me back off at home. Lily probably picked up on my energy, or *vibe*, as she likes to state, and knows that Rowan Harper is officially now an enemy to the Jones and Ballis household.

"You don't come here."

"Was in the neighborhood."

"Liar." This isn't the neighborhood a rich businessman would have a stroll in. He chuckles, coming to sit in the seat across from me. "No, no. I did not say you can sit with me."

"Didn't ask."

I roll my eyes and place my shaky hands in my lap, looking out the window. I consider leaving, but I was here first, and I can admit to being hardheaded enough to stand my ground. I can feel his stare burning a hole in the side of my face. "What?!"

"You're gorgeous."

Butterflies erupt in my lower stomach and instead of acknowledging them, I mentally take a sword and slice off their wings. "And you're odd."

He leans back in his chair, his knuckles gripping the wooden armrest. He turns his head sideways, looking deeper into the shop just as a blinding flash bounces off the window. I nearly jump from my seat after the proceeding *bang*.

Paparazzi.

His camera is covering the top half of his face, trying to snap a photo of us. "What are you doing tomorrow?"

I look back at Rowan, ignoring the pestering gnat—it's a little hypocritical of me, since it's my job to do the same. "Nothing that involves you."

The man continues to slam his hand on the window, pleading and mumbling to get our attention. Rowan scrapes his chair against the floor and walks to the opposite side of the café, exiting through the back door.

I look out the window and wave my hand to shoo the man away, but he snaps a photo of me, pulling his camera down with an evil grin. A motorcycle rumbles through the back alley before skidding through the traffic at an unsafe speed.

"Are you guys, like, dating now?" Lily asks, sneaking up to my side and also following the sight of Rowan's bike, weaving through traffic in the distance.

"Rather die."

"Will you finally tell me what happened the other day?" She sits down in the empty chair. "And why he was just here staring at you like he wanted to eat you whole?"

I roll my eyes, waving her off.

"No seriously, Celeste. You'd be his breakfast, lunch, and dinner."

"Aren't you on the clock?" I scan the surroundings to see if I can find her boss. "I'm not afraid to tell your boss you're harassing me."

She clutches her hand at her chest with a sharp gasp. "How dare you try to send that devil of a man after me. You know he hates my guts."

"Maybe because you're always late and never get orders right." I shrug my shoulders, picking up my coffee cup to hide my smirk.

"Sorry not everyone can be like you, Miss Perfect." She holds one finger in the air to stop me from whatever I was about to say. "Scratch that. You're not perfect." Her eyes squint in my direction. "Want to know why?" she intones.

"Wh—"

"Because I know for a fact that you haven't packed yet," she humphs.

I groan out loud, hanging my head off the top of the chair. Every year we go to Greece to visit

Lily's family. Her family became mine instantly when we first met, which I am very grateful for. I love the Ballis family. But every year, I always under-pack, which results in me digging through Lily's suitcase and Lily becoming irritated because my hips are wider than hers and I stretch out her jeans. Her words, not mine.

"Yeah, yeah, that's right, missy. So go home. And pack."

"I still have a few days!"

She points her finger at the door, her eyes closing and her lips pulling into a tight line. I throw my laptop back into my bag and grab my coffee. When my palm touches the door, I turn back to her. "Wait," I say, patting myself down until my hand goes into my pants pockets. "Oh!" When I pull my hand out, I give her the middle finger, quickly opening the door to run out of the shop to dodge the wet towel she throws at me.

CHAPTER TEN

ROWAN

I walk into Haper International, an all-glass building in the middle of the city. "Good morning, Rowan," our receptionist says. I told all our employees to call me Rowan, not Mr. Harper, so there is no confusion between my father and I. Lance had me when he was only eighteen, making him forty-seven. We could look almost identical due to our strong facial features, but the long hours in the office gave him extra years, extra wrinkles, and a patch of thick grey hair.

I press for the twelfth floor when I enter the elevator. As the door is about to close, they come to a stop around a briefcase. I raise my eyes from my phone to make direct eye contact with Lance. "Morning, Rowan," he says as he steps into the elevator, pretending to pick lint off his suit jacket.

Ignoring him, I look down at my phone, watching the live footage of Celeste dancing around in her room. I fight to keep my expression placid as she twirls in a circle with clothes in her hand, her mouth moving as she sings to whatever song is playing.

The elevator comes to a stop and Lance and I step for the door simultaneously. He takes a step back and waves his hand, offering for me to go first. I beeline to my office, slamming my door shut and sitting behind my desk. I drag my hands down my face, preparing myself to go through thousands of emails.

"What?" I yell when someone knocks on my door.

My door cracks slightly with Megan, our assistant, peeking her head in. "Rowan, Mr. Harper would like to see you."

"Tell him I'm busy."

"Yes, sir."

The elevator ride up here was enough close proximity for the day. I rarely come into the office, so the time I spend here cannot be interrupted with whatever bullshit he wants to spew at me. I open my laptop, seeing at least over twenty new emails with high importance tags on them. New contracts for me to review and forward to our accountant.

A knock interrupts the first page I start reading, Megan opening the door and holding a stack of papers tall enough to hide most of her body. "Rowan, Mr. Harper says you're not busy and to meet him now."

I stand out of my chair, pushing it far enough to crash into the window behind me. I button my suit, walking toward Megan. She tries to walk backward to get out of my way but ends up tripping on her extra high heels and the paperwork scatters on the floor at our feet.

She quickly bends down, scooping up the papers into a pile, mumbling, "Sorry." I bend to one knee to help her pick up the mess and make a mental note to send her an anonymous check. I'm sure Lance doesn't pay her enough, plus the overtime, hard work, and probably verbal abuse she goes through puts her constantly on edge.

Once she has the papers clutched to her chest, she gives me a quick smile before scurrying away. I turn to head down the hallway into my father's office. Not caring to knock, I swing his door open. "Whatever you have to say could have been sent in an email."

At the end of the day, I don't need this job. I *keep* this job because I don't trust Lance, and if that means putting up with him here just to keep my eyes on him while I look for my mother, then so be it. I do very well for myself with my company. My net worth is well over his, but he doesn't need to know that. My business is by word of mouth, and there are a lot of mouths in New York, but the only people who know about DWYM are the people who *need* to hear about it.

I stand behind the chairs in front of his desk, my hands bunched in my suit pocket. Lance looks up from his computer screen, his eyes immediately catching on the scar on the left side of my face. His lip curls in disgust, as if my scar is an inconvenience to him. "Sit down, Rowan."

Instead of listening to his demand, I walk toward the bar he has in the corner of his office, pouring myself a glass of his finest whiskey before I turn to face him.

He sighs, tugging on his reading glasses and pushing them through his locks to sit at the top of his head. "What I want to talk about is not smart to send in an email. So please, sit down."

I scoff, pouring myself another shot—or two.

"I would like to involve you in the next meeting."

I tip the decanter back up after almost overfilling the crystalware. Heat immediately burns at the tip of my ears, my knuckles around the glass turning pale. Does he know I'm searching his files? Searching for something that is not right within the company? Is he trying to play reverse psychology? Because there is no other reason for him to bring me deeper into the business unless he is catching on.

"Rowan, just sit. I think I have been holding back on you, and I apologize for it. You are more involved in the city then I am, and you would benefit me and the committee in the meetings."

My eyes bore into him while I slowly bring the drink to my mouth, sipping loudly. His index finger taps on the gold ring around his middle finger before he nervously starts twirling it. "Why did you give up?"

His lip curls, placing his hands on his thighs. "Give up?"

"Why did you give up on looking for Mom?"

He tucks his chin into his chest and sighs. "I never stopped looking for her, son."

I scoff, looking the other direction. *Son.* The word I hate hearing slithers so easily off his tongue. I despise being related to Lance Harper. A fucking quitter. A man who gave up searching for his wife. His love. I'd never stop looking if my wife went missing. I'd burn the land to the ends of the earth in search for her.

"That night—the night it happened—I told the cops about your mother's ex-fiancé."

"What?"

"I told the cops about how, ever since she left him at the altar for me all those years ago, she would get letters in the mail, death threats. Joan always said she felt like someone was watching her when she was out in town. But I told her it was because she was married to a billionaire." He lets out a short, husky laugh, pointing his chin high on his last statement.

I give him an empty look. I was never informed that my mother was engaged prior to Lance. My heart beats furiously in my chest, as if it could punch a hole through my ribs and launch free from its cavity. That changes things. That is a huge gap I missed in my mother's file for over three fucking years.

A prior fucking engagement.

I stand still, clenching my fingers. As a kid, I noticed my mother's skittishness, refusing to leave the house. As I got older, it got worse. I always thought it was because of my father's doing—his abusiveness, but now an ache in my head forming just beneath my left eye tells me there is so much more to my mother's disappearance that I am missing.

"After a couple of weeks, the cops said they couldn't find any traces of her ex. They think he left the country." Lance shrugs his shoulders, turning back to focus on his computer. "The meeting is next—"

"What was his name?"

A smile tips the corner of his lip. "Max… Max Hinderburg."

I set the filled glass down on his desk, knowing it will irritate his OCD. Without another word, I leave his office, hearing his demands bellow behind me about a meeting.

Fuck the meeting.

I slam my thumb into the elevator button, looking up to watch the numbers tick by. I pull my phone out of my pocket and text Jace, informing him to meet me now.

Twenty minutes later, I walk into Club Opal and find Jace already in our section. His blonde hair covers his forehead as he slams his fingers against his laptop's keyboard. I sit next to him and use my phone to log in to our system, both of us on the search for Max Hinderburg.

I can't trust the cops to do a full investigation, and I know for a fact that my software database is better than theirs.

Jace turns to me with a wicked grin, grabbing the handle of a vodka bottle, and takes a full chug. I wait for him in silence, one eyebrow levitating as he uses the back of his hand to wipe off the spill from the corner of his mouth. "I found a trace. He's not very good at keeping his digital footprint a secret."

Fire boils underneath my skin. A digital fucking footprint and the cops couldn't reach him? I lean closer to look at his computer screen. For the past three years, he has been staying in a hotel in Siena, Italy.

Biggest Fan

I pick up my phone and step to the back of the room. I finish my phone call in under two minutes and turn to Jace. "Meet me at my house in two days, he will be there."

He looks at me, his bright blue eyes turning into a dark hurricane. His smile is as evil as the Devil's himself. One thing about Jace is he loves a good *interrogation.*

Jace decides to stay at the club, probably to ogle the server he's been eyeing for the past three years. I could give less fucks about staying at that hideous club. We only work there because there are clients surrounding us. Stupid fucking men who need someone's head but can't find them. On rare occasions, we get a man whose wife took off with their money, and they hire us to find her and get their money back. Ten times out of ten, the wife took off for a good reason. When we catch up with the wife and she explains everything to us, we let her slide, and instead we teach the husband a lesson or two.

Mine and Jace's hands have more blood on them then anyone could imagine. For a normal person, it seems insane, but any normal person would go to the cops. I scoff, taking out my pack of Marlboros. I've seen firsthand what happens to a woman when she goes crying to the cops about what her rich, influential husband has done to her.

That's why me and Jace happily make sure that man doesn't do it to anyone else.

John holds a lighter to my cigarette. I nod to him, taking a drag and blowing the toxins to the left of me. John has been working for me for years, and he's never one to speak, much less offer me his lighter fluid. "What do you think about this Max?"

He shrugs his shoulder, turning his back to me to stand guard in front of the alley. I take another long drag, staring at the back of his broad shoulders and letting the ashes fall to the ground. This could be it. Max could be the answer to my mother. I flick the stick from my fingers, walking out of the darkness with a smile on my face.

CHAPTER ELEVEN
CELESTE

I hate flights. The turbulence, the cold air constantly blowing on your face, the uncomfortable seats, and so many people smashed into a tin can that can fly. To whoever created airplanes: I hope your pillows are warm every time you try to sleep. But the person who created airplanes is dead, so I curse their descendants with hot pillows. I hope they're never comfortable when they go to bed. Curse them.

"Stop putting witchy spells on the creator of the plane, Celeste," Lily whispers behind me.

"I curse them for eternity." We're slowly moving down the jet bridge. Every time I fly, I thank the universe for not allowing the tin can to drop from the sky. Lily thinks I'm dramatic, but humans were not meant to be over thirty thousand feet in the air.

This year in Athens is special. We are celebrating Lily graduating from school and being accepted into the NYU School of Law. She hasn't told her family yet, so I am grateful and excited to share this experience with them.

By the time we get to her house, I can smell her mom's cooking and hear her siblings running around the living room. All the things I wish I could have experienced myself growing up.

Her parents immediately sit us down at the table and start handing us food: taramasalata with flat bread, dolmades, calamari, and multiple grilled meats that I can't always distinguish but know their flavors will melt on my tongue.

Lily sits to the left of me with her parents in front of us, and her siblings surrounding in whatever space they can squeeze in as Lily shares her news. Her parents jump up in excitement and start chanting in Greek as they dance around the table holding hands. Mr. and Mrs. Ballis release each other from their grip and force us to jump up and down with them in a circle. The multiple slices of bread I have stuffed down my throat are making their way up my trachea, and I have to puff out my cheeks and hold my breath so I don't barf up Mrs. Ballis' cooking.

After a few minutes of dancing and forcing the saliva back down, Mrs. Ballis looks at me, inching her head to the side. "So, Celeste… where is your boyfriend?"

My neck snaps toward Lily, who already has her hands up in defense.

"Just because we don't live in America doesn't mean we don't see social media."

Lily's arms drop, both of us quickly running back to the living room to grab our phones. I can hear Mr. Ballis slamming his fist against the dinner table, mumbling, "There will be no boyfriends for my daughters."

"I found it." Lily's hand covers her mouth as she turns her screen to me. The photo is of me and Rowan sitting in the café. My head is tilted in amusement at him while he is looking in the other direction, smirking in the distance. A great photo that makes it look like we *like* each other. That we are having a great time in each other's company, but that was not happening. "Celeste?"

My heart beats faster than a hummingbird's wings, the pounds so furious it makes me want to crawl out of my own skin and collapse into a pile of bones.

"Earth to Celeste?"

That's what I'll become. A pile of bones. Nothing but a lifeless— "Ouch!"

"Well Jesus, I thought you were having a stroke."

"A stroke would be better than this."

"It's not that bad." She turns the phone to inspect the online magazine article. "New mystery girl spotted with New York's favorite bachelor Rowan Harper..." Her eyes continue scanning, wincing, until her lips fall flat and she locks her phone, throwing it behind her onto the couch. "You know what? It doesn't matter."

"What did it say?" I ask with an exacerbated sigh.

"What matters is us getting drunk." She grabs my shoulders, shimmying them. "Hotel. Dress. Drunk."

The Ballis home is small, and with her three little siblings, there's no room for extra guests. I always tell Lily I'm fine sleeping on the couch, or the floor—nothing I've never done before. But she demands we stay somewhere where we can unpeacefully come home at three a.m. without waking up the spawns of the Devil, aka, her siblings—her words, not mine. "Fuck it, let's go," I say, grabbing my suitcase, ready for a night to forget all about Rowan fucking Harper.

We got adjoining rooms this year. I drag my suitcase into mine and throw the luggage onto the bed. I snatch the curtains open to the floor-to-ceiling window, letting the sunshine into the room.

"Isn't this amazing?!" Lily says, dropping onto my bed and rolling around on the comforter. I sit next to her, pulling my phone out of my pocket and scrolling through the gossip articles.

It's pretty brutal.

One of them states I'm a nobody. A local stalker who is probably trying to feed off Harper's money. A pair of legs wide open for the king. The list goes on.

I turn around when Lily snatches the phone from out of my hand and throws it near the bedframe. "We will not indulge in the lies."

"They're kinda not wrong."

"Celeste Jones." Lily jumps in front of me, putting her hands on her hips. "You are not a fat whale."

"Fat whale?! One of them said that?!" I turn around to reach for my phone, but Lily grabs my shoulders to face me toward her.

"Listen. You're in this industry. You know the lies they make up. It's all for publicity and it will wash over sooner than later."

That's the issue. Publicity. Before I am even able to get my name out there myself, I get caught with New York's favorite drama stag and now my name is being dragged in the dust as a known slut rather than for my photos, or my art. Either people love him, hate him, or want to fuck him.

I currently hate him.

I take a deep inhale to try and push back the tears that are pricking my eyes. I moved to New York to run away from my past and make a name for myself. It's been a rough two years but now it really feels like it's all falling apart.

Lily wraps her arms around my neck, pulling me into her massive boobs and squeezing me tight. "Getting drunk will solve our problems," she whispers, causing me to chuckle into her shirt. She pushes me back before grabbing my hand and leading me to the mini fridge. She pops open the door and hands me a tiny bottle of Bacardi Coconut and takes one for herself. We crash the bottles together, hit them on the table, and tip our heads back, letting the shooters empty into our mouths.

Lily points to my suitcase on the bed and waves me off to get dressed. I immediately start rummaging through my clothes, knowing I brought some type of clubbing outfit. After a frustrated ten minutes of trying to put something together, I head toward the bathroom to shower and do my makeup.

Lily comes into the bathroom while I'm face-deep in the mirror, lining my waterline. She is brushing her teeth, but her other hand is holding a small black dress. She throws it at my face and walks away with her middle finger in the air. "Thanks!" I yell her way.

After an hour and a half, we are both finished getting dressed. The tight black dress Lily gave me extenuates my curves, and pairing the dress with red five-inch stilettos makes me feel like a runway model. Lily is wearing a black miniskirt and a white V-cut blouse that pushes her breasts up to her neck.

"God, we are hot! I called the cab," she says, fixing her lipstick in the mirror.

I take one last look, picking lint off my dress, then throwing back one more shooter of Bacardi. "Let's go."

"Hold up." Lily grabs a water bottle from the mini fridge, popping off the top and grabbing all our empty shooters. I stare at her with a raised eyebrow. "I ain't paying fifty dollars for each shooter." She winks at me while filling the mini bottles up with water and closing them back up, placing them into the fridge. "All good."

The cab pulls up to the darkest part of Athens. No streetlights, no building lights, just one big industrial warehouse with a red door that almost matches Club Opal. Lily holds my hand as we push through the crowd to the bar. "Two vodka Red Bulls," she says to the bartender.

I scan the club after making eye contact with two men sitting at the bar staring at us and whispering. Multiple people are on the dance floor, and every bar table surrounding the rest of the floor is occupied. There are stairs that lead to the top floor where people are leaning over the barrier, watching the rest of us.

The men who were staring and whispering scoot closer. "Let us buy you ladies drinks," one of them says in what could be a Russian accent.

"Great, take this tab." Lily pushes the receipt to the man, points to them while looking at the bartender, and grabs our drinks before pulling me away. All of it happens so fast it gives me whiplash.

"Where the fuck are we?!" I ask in Lily's ear over the vampire goth music. Lily stops us in the middle of the dance floor and starts syncing her hips to the music while I try to find the beat. I continue looking at the people around us, waiting for Blade to float from the darkness and start shooting this place down.

I take a sip from my drink, wincing at the large ratio difference of liquor to Red Bull. The music punches my ear drums and the vibration tickles its way from my toes to the pit of my stomach. My heart sinks with the bass. Lily pumps her fist in the air, finishing her drink. An odd vibration, bounces against my breast, off-beat to the music. I pull out my phone to see a new text message.

Unknown: Any man who dances with you is a dead man.

I scroll above to see the prior messages. This is the number I blocked days ago. I frantically look around the club to try and spot anything unusual, as if I am a detective and would even know what I am looking for. "Did you post us on social media today?!" I yell in Lily's ear, but she's already too far gone, already wrapping her hand around some random guy's neck.

Behind me, the stench of the subway during rush hour, mixed with that of a sweaty gutter rat, rubs against me. I turn around, placing my hand on the guy's chest. "No thank you," I say, trying to push him away. He grabs ahold of my wrist and shoves my arm in the air, his other hand gripping my hip and pulling me in. I try to lock my heels into the tile floor, but his hand overpowers me.

"Hey!" Lily shoves the guy's shoulder, throwing him off balance. "She said no, knock it off!"

The guy starts yelling at Lily in Greek and she responds back. I've never heard Lily speak Greek. Her family speaks it on occasion when we are here but… I look at the man who just tried to force himself on me. He's laughing at Lily before he shakes his head and walks away.

"Why was he laughing?"

"Pretty sure I called him a dumb pencil." Lily shrugs her shoulders and turns back to the handsome man who was patiently waiting for her.

I'm not a jealous person. Lily is a beautiful girl, but why is it that I get the men who smell like they haven't washed their balls in six weeks or the guys who are nowhere close to being attractive? Rowan is the only good-looking man who has ever paid me the slightest bit of attention and it's probably just because he ran out of supermodels and I was the first person who piqued his interest.

I squeeze through the crowd, making my way to the bar for another drink... or two. I grab the first empty spot and lean against the counter.

"Hi." A man on the right of me sits sipping his drink. He has bleach-blonde, short, shaved hair and is wearing a dark suit. Thick pink lips, bright green eyes, and a heart-shaped face. He turns to face me fully, showing the little dip right in the middle of his chin.

"Hi," I mouth, shuffling my weight on each foot. "Cran vodka, please," I ask the bartender, who looks severely overwhelmed. He turns around and slams his fingers on the computer before he shoves the receipt onto the counter.

I reach for my handbag to take out my card, my eyes returning to the counter to see money slapped onto the bill. I look at the stranger to see him grinning at me. "Dance with me?"

I nod, grabbing my drink without breaking eye contact. He softly takes ahold of my hand, bringing me back into the crowd.

The universe must have heard my complaints and cries because this man is handsome.

He places his hand on my hip, bringing his lip to my ear. "Is this okay?"

I nod my head ecstatically.

"You are beautiful."

I lock my knees to keep them from collapsing. He has an accent too? Lord, save me now. Lily is ahead on the right, dancing with someone new, but she turns her back on them, and when she spots me, she looks at who I'm with and gives me two thumbs up.

Colorful lights flash from the DJ booth. Smoke billows into the air and the ground shakes beneath our feet as the tempo changes, causing everyone to jump up and down. I feel great until I squint my eyes from the lights and try to reopen them. They feel heavier than before. The man in front of me says something once, twice, and I'm unable to catch the words. His mouth doubles, two side by side, before they merge into one mouth again.

I grab ahold of my stomach, feeling nauseated and tired. My knees weaken, buckling to throw me to the ground. An arm wraps around my waist to keep me upright and drags me from the crowd.

I try to clear my vision, but only darkness is ahead as my feet topple over each other. The club noises are muffled as my body is set down on something soft. Hands roam over me until a bright

light sparks in the room, followed by ringing in my
ears.

CHAPTER TWELVE
ROWAN

Death has a sound. When a cavity breaks, air hisses from the organs out of the mouth and releases a horrible stench that even my nose hairs can't help but curl away from.

I grip the pilers harder, bending the finger until it snaps. The cries bounce between the four walls until there is nothing left but whimpers. "It's been nineteen hours, and she still is not home," I say.

"Who?"

I grip the other finger, the ninth one. He has one more finger left to say something, or Mr. Hill will never be able to jack off again. He used to be Lance's accountant at the time of my mother's disappearance. He approved and denied all transactions on the account. Now that he is "retired," I expected him to be willing and cooperative, but it looks like even in his retirement, he is still loyal to Lance.

"Where could she have gone that she doesn't need return home for this long?" This finger snaps with ease. I peek up when Mr. Hill is too quiet. Seeing that he has passed out, I hold my hand out for Jace to give me the morphine. Feeling the syringe in my hand, I rip the cap off with my teeth and jam it into his thigh.

His eyes break open, along with his mouth as he gasps for air. Behind Mr. Hill lie two more bodies. They've been sitting in my basement, wrapped in plastic, for quite some time. They've expanded due to the heat down here, and I expect them to fully release their gases in less than three hours. One of them is the photographer who took and sold the pictures of me and Celeste. The other one is the one who wrote the dirty lies about Celeste in the magazine.

The last finger causes Mr. Hill to pass out again. With a sigh, I fall to sit on the concrete floor, my elbows resting on top of my knees.

"Are you asking about Celeste?" Jace questions, walking behind Mr. Hill to strap his arms back to the chair. "Because if so, she is in Athens."

"And you would know this because?"

"It's where Lily and her family is from."

I turn to John, who sits in the corner reading a news article. He sets the paper down in his lap and nods to me.

"Oh no, lad. You aren't leaving." Jace looks at the clock on the undecorated wall. "You have less than twenty-four hours before the Hinderburg package arrives."

"Finish him off and call the company to clean the rest up." I push myself off the floor, wiping my hands on Mr. Hill's jeans. John hands me a towel and I silently thank him before he makes his way up the stairs to the main floor.

"And if Hinderburg arrives before you? What am I supposed to do? What is ye even going to do when you get there? Say 'don't fucking block me again?' 'Ye ain't allowed to leave New York without me?' She's going to freak when she finds out you're stalking her." I catch Jace's terrible mimic of how I sound but I'll ignore it for now.

"You want to talk about stalking? How'd you know they were in Athens?" My brow raises in question. Jace's mouth opens before he quickly shuts it. "Keep Hinderburg busy. I'll be back in time."

It takes us nine hours to get to Athens. Nine. Fucking. Hours. As soon as I got off the plane, I follow her location to a hotel. John parks the car outside as we wait for movement. No music. No talking. Just me and John sitting in silence, staring at the three-star hotel doors. I haven't slept in forty-eight hours. Jace and I have been working non-stop on my mother's case, tracking down the reporters, paparazzi, and now Celeste Jones.

Just as I am about to close my eyes, I hear a laugh that makes all the surrounding noise in the city disappear. I lean closer to the window to see Lily and Celeste jump into a cab. John starts the car and cuts into traffic to follow, nearly hitting the pedestrians in the street.

The taxi stops after twenty minutes, dropping the girls off at a location I, myself, wouldn't want to indulge in. Theres no streetlights, no surrounding business with cameras. Just a large warehouse that looks perfect for criminals to do their business in.

John pulls off to the side and I watch the girls walk through the door, the club music blasting before it goes silent. I notice there's no guard at the door to check before you go in. I open the glove box and shove my Glock in my waistband before jumping out of the vehicle to follow them inside.

As soon as I enter, my lip curls in disgust. Every breath I take makes me want to carve my own skin off. I try to scan the crowd for a tall blonde girl and a short, curly-haired, brown-skin angel, but every inch of this place is packed.

I move from the entrance door, making a right to go upstairs. I don't want to ruin her night. I just want to make sure she's okay. That she's safe.

Biggest Fan

On the way here I reminded myself that I wasn't going to make myself known. That I'll just watch from a distance.

I find an empty spot, placing my hood over my head, and lean against the railing. I spot them at the bar, Celeste scanning the crowd with a pinched face. I wonder if she's thinking the same thing as me right now. That this place is disgusting and smells like a fish market. Or is she contemplating how to convince Lily they should go somewhere else? I'm begging her to convince her friend to go somewhere else.

My eyes catch every man who looks at them while Lily drags her to the middle of the dance floor. After a while, I slowly pull out my phone, never losing sight of her as I send a text.

"You from here?" a girl besides me asks. I ignore her because Celeste's just shoved her hand down her bra, bringing her phone out to stare at the text. Her face falls and I can see her eyes go wide as the strobe lights dance across her face. "Do you want to buy me a drink?" I wave my hand to try and shoo her away. "Oh c'mon. Don't be like that."

I turn my head toward her, making sure the side with my scar is visible. She blinks repeatedly, trying not to show her disgust before giving me a tight smile and walking away.

My eyes move like my scanning program, trying to find Celeste again. She's not in the same spot. I straighten my back, my fingers cracking against the metal rods. She inched her way into a corner, a man gripping her arm. Before my feet can move to dash downstairs and bash this man's face into his skull cavity, blonde hair appears and pushes him away.

He and Lily argue for a second before he walks away, leaving the girls alone. An inch of respect forms for Lily until she also walks away, leaving Celeste alone in the crowd once more. Celeste's shoulders drop, looking around until she finally drags herself back to the bar.

It takes every fiber in my body to not run downstairs and grab her myself. I let out an irritated grumble when my phone rings in my pocket. "What?" I use my other hand to shove a finger down my earhole to block out this obnoxious music.

"How is she?" Jace asks.

"You should come see for yourself." I stare at the blonde he is asking about. I figured he would call at some point. He doesn't talk about it but he has been obsessed with Lily ever since we got our membership at Club Opal.

"You're a fecking *gobshite*, you know that?"

I hang up on him, cursing at myself when I notice Celeste not able to hold herself up. Another man's arms are wrapped around her waist as he drags her down one of the hallways. I push through a group of people walking up the stairs. They curse and drinks spill everywhere as I take two steps at a time.

I knock over a few more clubbers as I stomp into the middle of their groups. I catch sight of the man pulling Celeste into a room and I run faster, my hand gripped on the weapon in my waistband. I reach the door they're behind, not wasting any time opening it, and quietly shut it behind me. He stands over Celeste, and without another thought, I lift my gun and pull the trigger.

CHAPTER THIRTEEN
CELESTE

Being in a hotel has such good perks: a heavy tucked blanket, pillows as soft as a cloud, AC so loud and so cold, the smell of bleach and fresh bed linens, the taste of vomit…

I groan internally and externally because why do I taste vomit? And why does it feel like the earth is spinning this fast? And why do I have a debilitating cramp on my left side?

I roll over to my other side, heaving before I jump out of the bed, tripping into the bathroom, and shove my head into the porcelain. I don't remember having that much to drink—actually, I don't remember last night at all.

My hair is pulled back from my face as I continue to dry heave.

Note to self: never drink again.

I shove my back against the tub, rubbing my hand across my mouth before shoving my palms into my eyes. I guess Lily decided to turn the lights on after I ran in here, which is really fucking rude. Bright lights and hangovers don't mix.

I slowly start to open my eyes, noticing a wide body, onyx hair, a scar, full lips— "What the fuck!" I lift myself off the floor, swaying on my feet before I regain some balance.

Rowan's eyes go wide before his face swipes the shock away, turning to his usual brood.

I shove my hands on his chest, trying to push him away. "What are you doing here?! Are you fucking stalking me?! Get out!" I continue pushing but he's double my size and has more than half my strength in one arm.

"Stop."

My arms plop at my side. "You're joking, right?" I move around him to stand in front of the mirror and Jesus Christ, I look a mess, but I see my reflection, which means I'm not dreaming or hallucinating. I notice the dry crimson drops splattered across my skin. My nose pinches as I watch my finger go to touch them, watching them flake onto the floor. Rowan comes to stand behind me, my eyes meeting his through the mirror. His dark hair is scattered across his forehead, purple rings outlining his eyes.

"Is this..." My eyes catch a twitch in his upper lip. I slowly start to back away out of the bathroom, my hands raise outward to keep him at a distance. "Please leave."

He shakes his head, stepping in sync with my feet. My back hits the foot of the bed frame.

"I'm not going to hurt you," he states.

"Then whose..." A flame catches in my throat as I try to figure out what is all over my skin. I raise my arms, turning them as I inspect.

"I'd never let a man harm a woman," he growls.

My arms fall, my hands gripping the bedsheets as Rowan stares at me. His dark eyes settle, turning softer with each blink. "I'm sorry I wasn't there sooner."

"Why? What happened?" I choke. "Where is Lily?"

"With John." The AC shuts off, silence billowing through the room. The sun barely shines through a crack in the curtain right in front of Rowan, but he stands back, hiding in the shadows. "You should shower, get some more rest."

"No." I wrap my arms across my chest. "Not until you tell me what happened."

Rowan walks to the corner of the room, sitting in the chair, and throws his hoodie over his head. "Shower."

I stand on my feet, swaying, and have to swallow the bile that rises in my mouth. "I want you gone when I'm out." I shuffle to the bathroom and slam the door behind me, immediately wincing when I lift my arms above my head to remove my shirt. I have to cover the gasp when I see the bruises around my shoulders. I close my eyes, taking a breath, trying to remember last night's events. Tears stream down my cheeks when nothing comes to mind. The last thing I remember is leaving the hotel and entering the cab.

Why can't I remember anything?

I enter the shower and goosebumps form on my skin before the heat seeps into my body. I watch the water turn ruby as it slides down the drain. More tears continue to slither down my cheeks as I continue to try and remember. I don't know if this is my blood, Rowan's, or someone else's, but I do know that whatever Rowan Harper did, I want no part of it.

I turn off the shower, wrapping myself in the towel. When I step back into the room, Rowan is still there in the corner. And honestly, I don't have the energy to care right now. As long as he stays in that chair—I'm assuming sleeping—then he can stay. Because whatever he did last night, whatever I did last night, I can't deal with right now. My head is foggy, my body is weak, and all I want to do is sleep.

CHAPTER FOURTEEN
ROWAN

The morning after the club incident, when Celeste got out of the shower, she crawled into bed naked. She must have thought I was sleeping, but after seeing her body still glistening from the water droplets—full thick thighs, a rounded ass, and a toned back—there was more than my back standing straight up. She slept eighteen hours straight. After six hours, I started to get worried and tried to wake her up, but she groaned, waved her hands, and turned her back on me. After eight hours, Lily's parents came banging on the hotel door, threatening to see Celeste. I had to *nicely* shut them the fuck up since she was still asleep and I promised I would get both of their "daughters" home safely.

When she finally woke, I sat on the large chair in the corner and watched her slowly pack her things. I texted Lily to start heading back to the hotel since I offered—demanded—that I take both of them home.

Nobody said a word to each other when John drove us to my private jet, or when we boarded and landed. Celeste stared out the window the whole time and Lily fiddled with her shirt, wrinkling the fabric to bits.

As I drive them home, Celeste sitting in the passenger seat and Lily in the back, Celeste stares out the window, her chin tucked into her hand. I wish she would say something. Did she put two and two together? Does she remember what happened that night? Either way, the fucker deserved much more than what I did to him. A shot to the head was too easy, too quick.

I pull to the curb in front of their brownstone. Lily exits the car and stands at the front passenger window, waiting. Celeste waves her off and I notice Lily's shoulders dropping before she walks up their stairs. She probably blames herself. As she should.

Celeste bites at her fingernails, looking out at the street in front of us. Her curls are in a loose bun on the highest point of her head. I catch sight of a purple mark on her shoulder when her loose shirt slides down her shoulder, and the fire burns throughout me all over again.

She reaches for the doorhandle and looks over her shoulder. "Thank you."

I wait until her front door closes behind her before I take off through traffic. I can't fathom the reason why I can't get Celeste Jones out of my mind. Since the night I saw her swinging from my trap. She has been consuming my every thought like a drug. It's infuriating. I didn't expect anything to happen in Athens. I wasn't going to make myself known, but I'm glad I was there. I'm glad she's monopolizing my mind. Because if she wasn't, who know what could have happened to her.

When I enter my house, Jace is sitting in the living room working on his laptop. I can see the irritation scatter across his forehead, probably because I said I was going to be quick, but the trip was almost three days, and Hinderburg arrived shortly after I left. "Where is he?" I take off my Santoni loafers, kicking my feet into my worn-out steel-toed boots. I grab the black T-shirt Jace left out for me, removing my hoodie to throw it on.

"Where else would he be, Harper?"

"I'll cut you."

Jace scoffs, throwing his laptop onto the couch and following me underneath the stairs to my basement door. I push the code into the keypad, opening the door and walking down the creaky wooden staircase. John is already here, in the far corner on the left, sitting in a chair, reading a magazine.

Hanging by the shoulders from two butchering hooks is Mr. Max Hinderburg. Sweat and blood drips down his face, pooling underneath his dangling feet. Jace rolls the tray of tools to us. Max's head twitches between his shoulders, his hands tied to the pole above his head, pulling them wide. His clasped ankles are spread apart and chained to the cement floor.

Either the cleaners didn't do a good job on their last appointment or Max already smells like death. I step up to our little victim, lifting his head to see his eyes roll to the back of his skull—correction, one eye rolls to the back of his head, the other one is swollen shut. Black and blue, and the size of a baseball.

I turn to look at Jace, who sucks on his teeth as he continues to polish the weapons. "You took too long, and he wouldn't shut the fuck up."

My fingers grip harshly on his chin, ripping the tape off his mouth. I take two steps back when his head falls between his shoulders again as he tries to spit blood at my feet. One wrong move and the skin attached to his shoulder blades should peel off his bones. I'd like to test this theory.

I hold out my hand out, Jace placing the pliers into my palm. I grab ahold of Max's chin hard enough to pop his mouth open, shoving the pliers in and grabbing his dry, brittle tongue. "Tell me everything you know."

He moans, his legs shaking, trying to get loose. I let go of his tongue but keep ahold of his chin, slobbered in drool.

"*Te ne pentirai,*" he spits.

I turn to Jace to see him shrug his shoulders. "Just because I'm Irish doesn't mean I know every language."

"I know. It's Italian, you dumb shit. I just—" I turn to look back at Max. I figured he picked Italy as his hiding spot, but him being Italian creates more questions. More problems. My mom is from Italy. Did she know Max for a long time? "Where is Joan?"

He doesn't respond, but I catch his facial muscles twitch into a smile. I pick up the butcher knife and swing at his wrist, cutting through skin, muscle, and bone like butter. His arm slips through the rope, falling at his side, his hand flopping into the pool of blood beneath his feet like a dead fish. His screams could be heard throughout the neighborhood if it wasn't for my soundproof insulation.

I grab a chair, turning it around so my arms can hang off the back, my legs spread wide, settling on each side. "I don't like repeating myself."

He silently cries, sniffling, moaning. His arm is cut clean, right at the edge of his wrist. He could probably get that reattached if I wasn't going to kill him. "You were engaged to her, were you not?"

John sighs in the corner, getting antsy like the rest of us.

"Over twenty years ago," Max replies.

"And my research says you haven't married at all. No kids. No wife. You still fond of Joan? Wish you still had her? Saw she got married to some New York prick and wanted revenge?"

"*Vaffanculo.*"

My eye twitches.

"What's that? What did he say? What does that mean?" Jace asks curiously, jumping at my side as I stare at Max. When Max lifts the corner of his mouth, I reach for the gun in my waistband, aim straight in the middle of his forehead, and pull the trigger.

One bullet. One bullet is all it takes to leave a gaping hole and brain matter splattered across the floor.

"Aw, man. What'd you do that for? What did he say?" Jace follows me up the stairs, both of us leaving the body to drain.

"Go home, Jace." I take off my shoes, throwing them out the back door connected to my open plan kitchen. I reach for a glass in my cabinet and pour a shot of whiskey.

"Well, I can't. Cleanup crew left for the week! Now I got brains to sweep up." Jace continues to mumble as he walks back under the stairs. I head in the opposite direction, out the front door, to sit on my patio with my glass.

Defeat swarms my body as I come to another dead end in this investigation. My chest tightens, body aching. I'm getting too old for this shit.

I set my whiskey down on the small table and pull out a cigarette. Every time I get more blood on my hands, I take the time to decompress outside. If I didn't, I don't think I'd be completely right in the head. I lose a part of myself with each kill, but sitting outside, smelling my large oak trees, the fresh dirt, it brings me back to reality.

When I was on a search for a house in the city, I tried to find somewhere that had distant neighbors and lots of land. I wanted to be able to see the stars at night, look up at the heavens and...

Heaven.

I take a deep drag, letting the ashes fall onto my jeans. There she is again, infiltrating my fucking head.

CHAPTER FIFTEEN
CELESTE

I throw the popped kernel toward my mouth and miss. It falls between the couch cushions with the rest of the badly aimed popcorn. Lily is next to me, her ice cream dripping down her wrist as she stares in shock at the current scene of TrueBlood. We've been stuck in the living room for a few days. I remembered what happened that night after Rowan dropped me off. It flooded my mind all at once and I broke down in Lily's arms. Since then, we've been having a little slumber party—wine, food, hogging who gets the blanket, who gets which side of the couch at night, and yelling at each other to move over because we have a foot up our asses.

Lily tried to apologize multiple times about that night, trying to take the blame. But it wasn't her fault. It's the sick men in this world who make me believe God should just wipe us all out. Who knows what he could have done to me and who knows how many other women he has done that to?

Lily's phone rings, and she instantly picks it up without looking at the caller ID. "Hi, Ma." I look toward her when she mutes the TV, her face scrunching together before her jaw drops, and she nearly breaks her neck to look at me.

"What?" I mouth.

"Ma, I'll call you back— No, no, Mom, we are fine— Yes, yeah, I'll call you back." Lily hangs up, throwing her phone on the couch, and jumps from her seat. "Girl!"

"What?!"

"Rowan fucking Harper killed that guy."

"What?" I set the popcorn bowl on the coffee table. Lily skips away, laughing into the kitchen, and grabs a bottle of wine. "Lily, what are you talking about?!" She pours a glass and scoots it toward the corner.

Lifting the blanket from my legs, I walk into our kitchen and sit at the barstool.

"That was my mom."

"Yes, I caught that."

"She said that she was watching the news, and that night, the club we were at, a man got killed. Shot in the head. You said the last thing you remember was a bright flashing light."

"The light could have been anything." I shake my head.

"C'mon, Celeste."

I grab the wineglass, chugging it. Rowan Harper is a murderer? The man who is constantly in the magazines, news articles, as being New York's favorite bachelor? Yes, he does have some rep—drugs, fights, supposedly jail time—but there is no way he would kill someone. I slam the glass down, my toes curling as the memories of me being trapped, hanging from his tree, fade in and out. It's odd to have traps set in your front yard, but to *actually* kill someone?

I take a deep breath, backhanding my mouth to wipe away the runaway wine.

"You should go ask."

"Are you insane?" Lily responds by shrugging her shoulders. "If that's true, I'm staying far, far away."

"At the end of the day, he saved you." Lily slaps both her hands on the counter, jumping up and down. "I know! Cook for him as like a little 'thank you for saving my life and possibly killing someone for me like a knight in shining armor.'"

I shake my head.

"C'mon!" she sing-songs. "You're so good at cooking and if it's true, which I'm betting money it is, he murdered a bad man. A man who could have hurt you. He's practically your savior. A Greek god sent down to save and fuck you raw." Her eyebrows bounce up and down.

"So now I'm selling my pussy again? He saved me so it's time to bust it wide open?"

She taps on her nose and points to me.

"You're sick."

"We're all a little insane, baby." She rounds the corner, grabbing my hands to pull me further into the kitchen. "Get to cookin'."

"Now? Don't you think it's late?"

"The Devil's spawns don't sleep."

I wrap my arms around my chest. "You're a little too enthusiastic for my liking about this whole situation. You do remember that he visits Opal and if I find out he's a killer, there is a high probability Jace is too."

"Yuck." Lily gags. "We do not speak of that name in this house." She walks away, taking my prior seat. "He's so annoying, always calls me Alan."

I use my hand to cover my laugh.

"It's not funny! Do I look like an Alan?!" She lifts her arms to the sides before they fall back down. "Now can you please cook something, go investigate, and maybe make extra?" She smiles fully with her teeth and squints her eyes.

I have to admit, I am a tiny bit curious to know if he really did it. And how he knew where I was and if it was him who was texting me from the blocked numbers. Once those questions form a list in my head, I turn around to open the fridge. I hear Lily say a little "yay" and clap her hands before returning to the couch. Is it smart to show up to a possible murderer's house? No, not at all. But if anything were to happen to me, at least Lily would know who did it and there would be justice.

It takes almost two hours for me to make jerk chicken, rice, steamed vegetables, and plantains. I plate it in Tupperware and thanks to me and my millions of food delivery jobs I've had in the past, I have a thermal bag to keep it all warm.

I look at the clock to see it's 2 a.m. Lily fell asleep twenty minutes into me cooking and I pray to the large woman above that Rowan is also not awake.

I thank the taxi driver and hand him some cash as I exit the vehicle. Standing in front of the gate, I look to my right and pass the brick wall. I can take a chance and possibly be trapped, or I can press the intercom and wake him up.

Or I can call the taxi back and leave like a sane person.

I press the intercom button, hoping that a housekeeper answers or I'll just be ignored and go back home. Advise Lily that I did my dutiful investigation and there was no murderer in sight.

As soon as I lift my finger off the button, the gate scrapes open. I watch as the hinges squeak until it stops wide open like the gates of Heaven. Or possibly Hell.

I take a deep breath and step one foot in front of the other, walking up the dirt and rock path. The closer I get, the more the house peeks from beyond the trees. The driveway wraps around a large fountain before bringing you to the Southern-inspired porch. There are no lights indicating that someone is home or even awake, so I quickly run up the stairs and place the bag at the door.

"Ah!" I scream when I turn around and find a shadow in front of me. I back up, my eyes quickly closing before opening again to see portions of his face hidden in the shadows with a cherry-red light bobbing from his mouth.

"What are you doing here?"

I look up at his eyes, exhaustion showing even more than the last time I saw him. He takes a drag of his cigarette before removing it from between his lips and blowing the smoke at my face. The darkness engulfs his body, not showing where his wide shoulders end. He leans around me, looking at the bag I just placed down. He picks it up, looking inside before focusing on me again.

"I guess it's a thank-you dinner. It was— I don't…" His brows scrunch together, and I would like the earth underneath my feet to open up and swallow me whole. My tongue is heavy and dry behind my teeth.

Biggest Fan

My thighs tense when he takes a step toward
me. He grabs my hand and opens his front door.
"Come. It's cold." I lock my feet in place, jerking
when he tries to pull me through the threshold. He
takes the cigarette out of his mouth and flicks it past
the porch.

A light somewhere deep inside his house
reveals to me a sinful act splattered across the chest
of his shirt, my eyes glued to the blemishes. His
eyes mimic mine, looking at the ruby stains
clashing against the white fabric. My heart pounds
against my chest, my brain telling me to run, but my
nervous system has a mind of its own.

Our eyes meet and his lip twitches into a
grin. "Scared?" He steps forward until I can smell
the iron mixed with a sweet musk and cigarette
scent. His lips are close to my forehead. "Run if
you're scared. Run and don't come back."

"You were stalking me and now you're
telling me to run?" I say, breathless.

"Maybe I like the chase." His arm wraps
around my waist, reversing our positions so that he
is behind me. He shoves me through the door, a
yelp leaving my mouth as I stumble in. I feel his
heavy presence behind me as he shuts us in. The
sound of a deadbolt makes my shoulders hitch into
my neck. When he walks past me to the right and
into his kitchen, I stand by the door, my mind
telling me to turn around, run down the driveway,

and never come back, but instead I stand in awe of the inside of his home.

It's a large living room with a black leather sectional and a TV hanging above the fireplace. The walls are white with swirls of light gray, giving it a marble wash. The floors are marbled white and gold. A black metal staircase leads to the upper level, but a dark hallway underneath the stairs sends chills against my skin.

The sound of liquid pouring into a glass interrupts my visual tour. Rowan nods for me to come in as he pushes a glass of wine across his kitchen island. I hesitantly approach, sitting down at the barstool. The wine I drank earlier still pools at the bottom of my stomach, giving me warmth, but being in this house with Rowan turns that heat into ice. It's extremely bland in here—no family photos, no lights, no life.

My hand grips the base of the wineglass, watching as Rowan floats around the kitchen. He pulls out two plates and silverware, removing my food from the bag and making us both a plate. When he hands me mine, I stare at it with wide eyes. Under his fluorescent kitchen lights, the crimson stains become more visible. His eyes meet mine—dark onyx eyes, gaping into my soul. Purple and green marks are under them, his hair messy as if he just woke up or has been constantly running his hands through the dark locks.

Murderer.

His chest inflates before he drops the plate on the counter in front of me, turning away to wash his hands. He leans over, splashing water on his face. He cuts the water with force and grips the edge of the ceramic sink, his blue veins popping on his forearms. My thighs twitch in my seat. His head snaps up, staring at my reflection through the window, and a tight smile forms on his face. Standing tall, he takes off his shirt and now I start to squirm.

What the fuck is wrong with me?

His body is covered in tattoos from his lower back to the top of his shoulders. He slowly turns around and my eyes follow the double dragons that whip around the nape of his neck to his Adam's apple. More obscure drawings continue low on his hips, showing off his perfect V.

"You made this?"

I nod once, clearing my throat as I stare into the wine, skeptical that he drugged it. My hand shoots back when Rowan snatches the glass away from me and takes a large chug. He places it before me and tops it off.

He leans with his elbows propped up, cutting the chicken to bits, scooping up some rice, and shoves it in his mouth. His eyes soften as he chews, and I have to bite my lip to keep from smiling. A shot of dopamine is injected straight into my heart as I watch him shove more into his mouth.

Remembering I have my own plate, I follow his lead, diving into my own food. The only sounds between us are the scraping of our forks against the plates.

A door is heard opening and closing, the sound of multiple deadbolts following. I gaze at Rowan to see him unfazed before I stare out of the kitchen, waiting to see who else is here.

A girlfriend?

His father?

A secret wife?

My heart slows when I see John turn the corner, my stupid heart jumpstarting when I notice him wiping his bloody hands on a pristine white towel. "All done, Mr. Harper."

"You're dismissed." I look toward Rowan, whiplashed back when I find him already staring at me. My lip curls when I alternate looking between Rowan and John and push my plate of food away. I take a sip of wine and look in my peripheral when the tapping of a keyboard enters the room. Jace stands near John while his face is inches away from his computer, and of course, he is also covered in blood.

Great, just one big bloodbath and I'm here, possibly the next victim.

"Miss Smith's case is handled but I'm still looking for more information on Max. Maybe if I—" Looking up from his laptop, Jace examines me, Rowan, and the food in front of us. "You're having a fucking dinner date and ye didn't care to invite me?" He walks closer and I lean away on instinct. He points to my plate. "Ye going to finish that?" When he first walked in, there was no accent, but now it's harsh and bold and I can't decipher if it's Irish or Australian.

I push my plate to him and he immediately starts eating my leftovers. "Sorry, Celeste. I'm fucking starvin', yeah. I'm Jace, by the way," he states with a full mouth. I've only ever heard of Jace from Lily constantly complaining about him, but now that I see him in person, up close, he is so Lily's type. Athletically built, golden blonde hair, ocean blue eyes, and skin overrun by tattoos.

"Cut the accent. You're dismissed, too." Rowan stands at full height, his brows overshadowing his eyes.

"Oh fuck off, Rowan. This is fucking delicious!" Jace drops the fork and shoots his hands in the air before slapping them down. A tick in Rowan's jaw is all it takes for Jace to roll his eyes. He snatches the plate from the counter. "Fine. But I'm taking this with me. Nice to see you, darlin'." He swivels around, following John out the front door.

My shoes tap at the leg of the stool, silence wafting between Rowan and me before I quickly state, "I should go too." I was here long enough to give him a thank-you and I think I have my answer whether Rowan is a murderer or not. I also should have assumed the wine he gave me is probably the strongest on the shelf, nothing compared to the cheap ten-dollar wine me and Lily keep in our house. I can feel it burning at my nerves, my body becoming too lax with the mixture of sleep deprivation.

I jump from my seat, but a hand lands gently on my arm. "Stay."

"I don't think that's a good idea."

"And why is that?" Confusion is written all over his face as if I don't know he is a murderer, as if the first time we officially met I wasn't hanging from a tree trap he installed, or that he stalked me to a different country.

He looks me up and down, heading to a closet between his kitchen and hallway. I run my clammy hands along my sweats, turning to look at the back door in the kitchen.

I can make a run for it...

Rowan hands me a pair of boxers and a large T-shirt. "You shouldn't be getting in cars with strangers this late at night. You can wear these."

"Staying at a stranger's house is any better?"

"I'm not a stranger." He puts his hand on my lower back, pushing me out of the kitchen and in front of his stairs. A magnetic shockwave flows through my muscles from his fingertips, asking for more. *Needing* more. My body becomes a fucking traitor to my own safety as he guides me up the foyer and leads me into a room.

A California king bed takes up most of the space. The bed itself is the size of my room but there's nothing here besides the bed, a dresser, and an en-suite bathroom.

My assumption that it's a guest bedroom is incorrect when he walks toward the dresser and drops his jeans down his thighs. I quickly turn around, giving him privacy with his clothes still in my hand. I'm mortified when I peek around my shoulder to see him in gray sweatpants, no shirt, and his arms crossed over his chest. I spin around and tuck my chin.

I have two options. Option one: I can stay here and possibly be murdered. Or option two: I can run out of here, screaming like a banshee, and move across the country. Change my name. Become a sheep farmer. I wonder if Lily would join me? I'll let her name all the—

"Do you need help?" I pivot, finding Rowan smirking at me, standing in the same position. "I assume you know the concept of changing clothes before bed?"

"Don't be an asshole."

"Don't be a pussy. I'm not going to hurt you. I thought we established that."

"You established that before I understood what the fuck you were talking about—"

"Dirty mouth."

I make an undefinable sound, somewhere between a moan and a gasp. "And then I come here, and you guys are all covered in blood!" My tone is coming very close to that of an ignored child having a tantrum. He pulls the tucked sheets out of the corners and lies underneath them, his hands behind his head. "I'm not sleeping with you."

"No choice. No guest bedroom."

"Go sleep on the couch or something."

He turns on his side, his head in his hand. "Do you know how much that couch cost? It's for looks. Not to sleep on."

I squint my eyes at him and he gives me a tight smile before flipping on his back. I walk to the bathroom and see there is no door for privacy. Fucking great. Setting the clothes down on the counter, I make a motion with my hands, imagining that I'm choking him out, a silent scream falling from my lips.

You could still just leave, the little angel on my shoulder tells me, and she's not wrong. I could leave. But if I'm being honest... I don't want to. I want more information on Rowan. I want to know why he was in Greece with us. I want to know why he won't leave me alone, and I want to know why when he touched me, I felt... different.

I fold my clothes and leave them and his boxers on the counter, walking back into his room with the T-shirt he gave me hanging below my knees. I point to him. "Touch me and die."

He crosses his heart and closes his eyes.

As soon as I get into bed, my body relaxes. This is the softest bed I have ever laid in. I stay as far toward the edge as I can, my back facing him. I bite my lip as I think of how to start my list of questions.

Chapter Sixteen
Celeste

I wake to the sun shining in my face, my body engulfed in warmth and— My eyes break open, seeing two dragons staring at me, and I'm hit with the smell of fresh linen, musk, and cinnamon. Rowan's arm is wrapped around my shoulder, my face is in his chest, and my legs tangled with his. "Oh shit," I whisper. I slowly untangle us and slide off the bed, landing with a soft *thump* on the floor.

"Shit. Shit. Shit." I quietly run to his bathroom, throwing off his shirt and putting my clothes back on. I pause halfway out his room when he stirs, rolling over with a pinched face. Even in his sleep, he doesn't seem relaxed. I snatch my phone from the dresser, seeing I have sixteen missed calls and twelve text messages from Lily. And Jesus, it's almost 3 p.m.

I scurry down the stairs, almost tripping, my hands gripping for the railing when I see John on the couch. "Miss Jones." He nods toward me.

Great, he probably thinks me and Rowan fucked. I haven't had a walk of shame in years. I give him a half smile as I unlock all the deadbolts on the front door, tensing my jaw as I hear the chains and links.

Finally outside, I pull out my phone and order an Uber as I walk down the driveway. The gate automatically opens and lets me through. I listen to all of Lily's voicemails while waiting for my driver.

Girl it's 7 a.m. Where the hell are you?

I'm still drunk from last night and I have work at eight. Call me back so I know you're okay.

Bitch I swear to God, everyone knows you pull out your phone after sex. Call me back!

Then there are multiple text messages throughout the morning and on her lunch break. I reply to her saying I'm okay and put my phone back in my pocket.

After the Uber drops me off at home, I immediately go to my room to lie down. I pull out my phone and send a question mark to my boss, switching back and forth between the message and my bank app. I need a new event, and soon, if I'm going to keep my account out of the negatives.

"Celeste Jones!" The front door slams and I jump out of bed, peeking my head out the door to see Lily looking around the house. Once she spots me, she starts beelining to my bedroom. "You little witch! Where the hell have you been?! Tell me everything, every dark little dirty secret."

For the next half an hour, I watch Lily get dressed in my room for the club while I tell her everything and nothing at the same time.

"That's it? No sex?"

"Nope," I say as I clean out my paintbrushes.

"Did you want sex?"

I contemplate her question. Rowan Harper is an extremely attractive man. A man that everyone in the city wants and a man I can't have. *Or trust.* And also, I cannot forget the most important part, hate. I'm sure the woman Rowan will marry will be his little naive housewife, a big ring on her finger she can barely keep up, and his kids on her hip. According to my OBGYN, a kid does not seem to fit into my future unless I want to go through multiple medical procedures and hormone therapy. Shout-out to polycystic ovary syndrome for taking away my rights to naturally produce. Plus, my main focus, my main goal, is my career. Getting my name out there. Be someone. Become someone. After everything I have gone through, I deserve the chance to show the world who Celeste Jones is. And Rowan Harper does not align within my stars.

"Earth to Celeste?" Lily snaps in my face before sighing. "Next time you go missing, call me at least, or send a fucking text." She kisses me on the cheek and sways her hips out of my room, the front door closing and locking behind her.

Biggest Fan

Rowan

I lie in bed staring at my ceiling with an empty pit in my stomach. She's gone. She left and didn't wake me as if this were some type of one-night stand. My pillows still smell of honey, my sheets like cinnamon and maple syrup.

I rub my hands over my face and grip at my chest. My heart is beating at an unstoppable pace. Swinging my legs off the side of my bed, I make my way to the bathroom and turn on the shower. I stare at my shirt that I gave her last night, bunched on the floor near my feet. The shirt was a dress on her delicate body, hanging down to her knees. I pick it up off the floor and bring it to my nose.

Cinnamon.

Maple syrup.

Honey.

My eyes close as all the blood rushes down to my cock, waking it up before I can even have my shower. With a grumble, I throw the fabric back on the floor and open the shower door. The steam immediately flows out, the water burning against my skin. I turn the knob to ice cold, but it still doesn't take the need I have for Celeste Jones away.

A scared, curious woman who has no filter. One who likes to talk back, challenge me.

I grip the base of my cock, squeezing it with a plead to go soft. I grunt when her face appears in my mind, her soft plush lips matching her plush curls. Her big brown eyes complementing her brown skin. A bead of cum drips from my head as I start to stroke. She fell asleep as soon as her head hit the pillows. Didn't wake when I pulled her body toward me, her legs shimmied into mine, her ass in my crotch, and all I wanted to do was flip her on her back and tuck my head between her legs. I wanted to hear her scream my name, beg me to stop and keep going. I wanted to see how far I could push her and how much more she could take.

My free hand hits the shower wall when my strokes become erratic. I envision her eyes filled with tears, her lips bruised and swollen as I fuck her pretty mouth then bite at her raw lips.

My cum spurts and drains with the rest of the water, my forehead hitting the wall as I suck in a breath of air. I turn the shower off, wrapping my lower half with a towel. My phone vibrates on the bedside table.

"Morning, handsome. Sleep well?" Jace teases on the line. My hard-on dissipates even faster hearing his voice. "You know that's why you're so fucking ugly, you never get your beauty rest. A good night's sleep, and a good skincare rout—"

"What the fuck do you want?" I put him on speaker, grabbing my clothes from the dresser.

"Well, while you were having *company,* I took it upon myself to, you know, focus on the very important job we have. I emailed you some more information on Miss Smith's case." Poor Miss Smith. Her husband—or now her late husband—was stealing money from her account to satisfy his own selfish needs. His nice addiction at Club Opal with drugs and the servers, along with his mistress, was crumbling his business. Miss Smith has her own elegant, highly recommended beauty parlor in New York and Mr. Smith thought she wouldn't notice a few hundred grand missing. When she found out and confronted her husband, he sued her for defamation during their divorce.

Now Mr. Smith is *missing,* and Miss Smith has all her money back and accounted for from the secret bank account her husband was hiding in a different country.

I make my way to my office, opening my laptop to see the ten million dollars added to our DWYM account and the twelve-page breakdown of the Smith file.

My phone call ends with Jace, his face pops up on the corner of my screen when he logs into our program. "I did more digging on Max."

I open the file to see notes scattered from the day he was born until the day he died in my basement. He grew up two streets down from my mom. They went to the same schools together, and if I'm reading this right... "Does that fucking say—"

"Yep."

Harper International. The co-owner of Harper International. How does that even happen? My mother was engaged to Lance's business partner? Jace pulls up an old wedding invitation, dated the same year I was born. Information my father could have easily given me of before I made a straight fool of myself in the basement, asking Max questions I should have known.

"What would you like me to do? I can try to find more details. I got a couple of lads who might be able to get into some old security systems at the office." Jace continues spilling options, but the only thing running through my mind is how this information somehow eluded me for so long. Key information that Lance kept from me.

I run my hands over my face. "Put a pin in it. We'll come back to this later." I shut the laptop and continue sitting in the dark. The house is silent, which is something I am used to by now. Growing up, the house was never silent. Lance was always screaming, bitching, abusing. But now, the silence is eating me. Swallowing me whole. I shift my legs in the chair to get more comfortable and when I continue to find myself not at peace, I slam my chair back into the wall and close my office door behind me. I continue down the hallway underneath my stairs and enter the garage, grabbing my keys for my MTT 420-RR and opening the garage door.

My bike is the only thing that is going to get me through the city's traffic. I let the bike drive itself, unsure of where I am going, what I am doing, until I pull into a convenience store. I take my helmet off and stride in. Bouquets of flowers are right at the entrance and I hesitantly walk toward them, eyeing each bouquet, not knowing which to pick. Roses seem too corny. Sunflowers look like they are already dead, drooping down to the floor. Lilies smell like baby powder.

"Well, if it ain't Rowan Harper."

I turn my head over my shoulder to see Brittany McLauren.

Fucking shit.

I grab a bunch of random flowers and walk to the cashier.

"Who are those for?" Her heels clack against the tile as she catches up to me, cutting me off in line and looking me up and down. She smells like she is wearing old lady perfume, chewing her gum with an open mouth, her hand on her hip. I keep my head above hers, staring at the line ahead of us.

A few years ago, Lance tried to arrange a marriage between us. He said, "Rowan, she's a good girl, a *sexy girl* and her parents taught her well. She is going to inherit her family business, and her finances will line up with yours. Your mother would be proud."

I would throw my head through a wall if I had to wake up every morning to see a plastic Barbie for the rest of my life. And my mother wouldn't be proud. She would want me to marry someone I love. Not marry someone just because they fit into my father's social standing requirements.

"Same old Rowan, I see." Brittany scoffs, shoulder bumping me as she walks away. *Thank fuck.* She never stopped trying. Even tried to propose to me. The few dates we went on, I sat quietly, not saying a word to her while she blabbed about the unnecessary fucking drama in the celebrity world. Who was cancelled, who was hitting on who, he-said she-said bullshit. I paid for our dinners and got her an Uber each time.

I pay for the flowers, grabbing a pack of chocolate bars in line, and shove everything in my backpack.

CHAPTER SEVENTEEN
CELESTE

My bed once again is covered in paint. Red and black. A mixture of grief and hope. I started this painting after I scrolled through social media to find another school shooting that happened this afternoon. Another tragedy in this world and no one seems to understand the issue at hand. My strokes become harsh, rapid, the angrier I get. My music contradicts the tears streaming down my face and the blood boiling beneath my skin.

I've been a victim of violence. My childhood was full of such events, as were the childhoods of the kids I roomed with. One by one, they disappeared, whether it was by their own hand, violence in the streets, or abusive foster parents.

We were kids.

They were kids.

I sit back, staring at the bleeding heart, my head tilting, fingers twitching.

"It's beautiful."

"Thanks," I say, looking over my shoulder before resuming my own critique of my work. I double-back and scream, jumping over my painting to the opposite end of my room, away from Rowan. "What the fuck are you doing here?!"

He holds out flowers and a whole box of Twix chocolate. A soft expression is smoothed on his face, his chest quickly inflating and deflating. Is Rowan Harper nervous? I walk around my bed and take his gifts. "How did you get in?"

He looks everywhere but at me, walking to my bed and staring at my new work. "You going to sell it?"

"Think so. But I'm donating all the profit."

He turns back to me, his eyebrows scrunching together. "Why?"

I scoff at his question. He and his family have probably never donated in their lives. I set the flowers and chocolate down on my bedside table. "The families from the recent incident made a GoFundMe."

"The recent shooting?'

I nod and he studies me with enough intensity that my knees buckle. "You never answered my question." I walk around him, grabbing my painting to set it on the easel to dry.

"Can I take you somewhere?"

I arch a brow. "Why?"

He shuffles on his feet. "Well, you snuck out of my house before I had time to make us breakfast."

"Make us breakfast?"

He nods. I imagine Rowan Harper in the kitchen cooking, sleepy eyes, frazzled hair, no shirt on, and his pants low on his hips like last night. I have to bite my inner cheek to keep from smiling. "Fine." I hold up a finger. "But I swear, Rowan. This is the last time we interact. I dropped dinner off last night as a thank-you. If you keep stalking me, I will call the police."

He smiles, grabbing my finger that is still pointed at him, and drags me out of my room. "Sure." His large hand covering mine sends chills up my arm and into my chest. I pull my finger from his grasp once we exit my house and spot a motorcycle parked on the sidewalk in front of my steps.

"Oh no. I am not getting on that."

He grabs the helmet on the seat and hands it to me. "Yeah, you are."

I push it back into his chest. "We can take my car."

He presses the helmet back, grabs me by the nape of my neck, and pulls me close to him, his helmet the only thing keeping our bodies apart. "Get on the bike, Celeste."

Before I know it, the helmet is over my head and my thighs are wrapped around him. His bike rumbles to life when he kick-starts it and takes us into traffic. I lay my head on his back and wrap my arms tightly around his stomach. My eyes shut tight when he swerves between cars and I have to hold in a scream when I think we are getting too close to another vehicle.

Every time we hit a stoplight, his gloved hands tap on mine. I'm unsure if it's his way of telling me we are alive or if I should let up on how tightly I'm squeezing him. Either way, I'm not letting go. If I fall, I am taking him with me.

After what feels like an eternity and a half, my body is almost launched off the seat when he drives over a bump to take his bike on the sidewalk. I lift my head, peering over his shoulder to see people scatter like roaches while he pulls up to a food truck.

He helps me off the bike, my legs shaking like a newborn baby deer, and removes the helmet from my head. "Was that fun?"

"No. You're crazy." I fix my curls, raking my fingers into my scalp to shake out the possible helmet hair.

"You can handle it." He takes my hand, dragging us to the front of the line as people whisper and try to sneak a photo.

"My favorite customer! Everyone move and make room! Rowan, get your ass up here!" the man in the truck screams. He leans out the window, opening his arms for Rowan to hug him. And I'm surprised when Rowan actually leans in to oblige.

Seeing him outside of his house, not around his co-workers, is a reminder that he is human. Not just a famous man everyone drools over. The man in the magazine is standing right next to me, holding my hand. My hand that is currently twitching to have him release his grip, but every time I try to pull away, he only squeezes tighter.

I peer over my shoulder, seeing a group of girls giggle and whisper to each other. Sweat develops at the nape of my neck and regret starts to build in my head.

"It's so good to see you. And you brought a beautiful young lady?! Did pigs start flying?" The chef looks at me, then up to the sky. His New York accent is strong, Brooklyn-like. Salt and pepper hair peeks out from underneath a hairnet and burn scars are scattered along his hands.

"I thought you already knew how to fly, Calvin?" Rowan laughs when the chef stretches out the window to try and strangle him. "Let me get two bacon, egg, and cheeses. Double wrapped and fried." Rowan reaches for his wallet in his jeans, turning to me. "I promise you're going to love this." He slams money on the counter, the chef kissing the hundred-dollar bill before waving us off.

I can't counterclaim that I won't love this. The smell coming from the small kitchen wafts around the area already and it makes my stomach gurgle. Food is a way to my heart, especially breakfast, but I won't tell him that. Cooking food, eating food, learning the history of food… It doesn't matter. There is something warm and comforting about it, then you add a person to enjoy it with you...

Rowan takes us to a bench on the side of the truck while we wait. "Don't worry, they will get their food too."

"They all might want you more than the food," I scoff.

"Can we add you to that list?"

"Maybe when pigs fly."

He snickers, looking over his shoulder toward the crowd. "You'll never get used to it," he tells me, setting his arms on the table and shrugging his shoulder when he looks back at me. "It's exhausting."

I believe him. His tone is sincere enough to slap me in the face. He is constantly belittled online just as much as he is worshipped, and I work in the industry that does both. Which makes me wonder just how much he will open up to me and why he even wants to be around me in the first place. My boss had messaged me a few pop-ups they received of celebrity outings and instead of immediately getting into my car, I picked up the paintbrush.

Yes, my bank account absolutely hates me.

Our burritos are delivered to us wrapped in foil. We both unravel our breakfast and my mouth instantly waters. "How did you hear about this place?"

"This was my mom's favorite spot."

I take a bite of my burrito and have to instantly put it down, clapping my hands and nodding. The crunch, the cheese pull, it's delicious. It's perfect and I'd like four more of them to go. "Well, tell your mom thanks for putting us on, this is really good."

"I'll tell her once I find her." Rowan takes a bite of his burrito and mine almost falls out of my hand. *Once I find her?* I stare at him, waiting for the details. Waiting for him to go more into depth, explain his sentence. But as he continues to take bites of his burrito, I come to the conclusion that I am going to have to ask.

"W-what do you mean?"

He wipes his hand with a napkin, then his mouth, chewing slowly to bring me to the edge of my seat. Teasing me in ways I don't want to be teased.

"My mother went missing three years ago. I created a coding program and named it Do What You Must—DWYM, for short—to find her. It's a private investigation program that allows me into anything and everything. Once I got it going, my program quickly turned into a company. Jace and I started to take on cases, helping women get away from their shit-for-brain husbands, and it keeps me somewhat at bay from my father's company."

I blink fast, trying to process.

"I come here to reminisce. Plus, these are fantastic breakfast burritos." He laughs before clearing his throat. "Before my mother disappeared, Calvin was telling her that his wife was sick and only getting worse. So, once a week I come here and overpay for my breakfast. At first, he tried to refuse when I would hand him the cash, but when he started to kiss the money and became extremely grateful, I knew I had to investigate his wife's condition." He shrugs. "Now his wife's medical bills disappear from a few donations here and there."

Great, now my assumptions of Rowan being a self-centered prick has dissipated into a million pieces. He created a whole business wrapped around his missing mother? Helping women? Paying people's medical bills? *The* Rowan Harper.

I place my hand over his and give it a tight squeeze, not knowing what to say. He stares at my hand on top of his, his brows lowering to cover his dark eyes.

I clear my throat and drag my hand away. "So, I'm assuming you do what you have to do with your company, as in…" I'm afraid to say it out loud, remembering last night how everyone was covered in blood. It's like they are some odd, morally grey vigilantes.

He nods.

"But they are, like, bad people, right? Like really bad?"

"I think the guy in Greece was bad."

I bite my bottom lip, looking in the other direction. Lily was right.

"Meet me tonight," he states. No question.

"Excuse me?"

He gets out of his seat, throwing away his foil and snatching my half-eaten burrito to place in his thin bag. I follow his lead right back to his bike and he puts his helmet over my head. Lifting the visor, he grabs ahold of the chin guard, pulling me close to him. "Meet me at Club Opal."

I push him away, scoffing. "Stupid, you know I can't get in."

"I'll get you in. Just come."

"Why?" I ask, both my hands still on his chest, keeping him at a distance even though his hand still grips the helmet.

I can see his facial expressions switch as he thinks of an answer—confusion, shock, fear, sadness, a mixture of all of them—before he says, "I want to be around you."

Chapter Eighteen
Celeste

"I want to be around you? That's the best he could come up with?" Lily is already dressed for work and is currently dressing me. She told me jeans and a T-shirt is too casual to even step foot in this club. Along with telling me no on my makeup. Now I have black liner on the bottoms and tops of my eyes—which I can't complain too much about, because it does make my brown eyes look golden. "He is really bad at flirting."

"I don't think he was flirting with me." I push Lily's hand away. She was inches from putting a bold red lipstick across my lips and that is where I draw the line.

"He can't even come pick you up for the date?"

"Not a date." I grab my purse and walk out my bedroom door.

"Then what do you call it?" Her heels clack on our floors as she catches up to me, cutting me off from the front door with her hands on her hips.

Biggest Fan

I shake my head, shoving her away. "Let me just get this over with."

I surprisingly find parking not far from the club. Lily is still teasing me while we walk on the sidewalk that this is definitely a date, and that Rowan definitely likes me.

A deep voice cuts in. "This *is* a date."

Lily screams, falling into me. Rowan creeps out of the dark from the alley next to the club.

"Not a date," I tell him.

"You have all this money in this world, and you bring her *here*?" Lily rolls her eyes, waving us off before she heads down the alley to enter the club through the back.

"Not a date," I reiterate. He looks down at me, his white button-up undone at the top, his hands in his slacks, and his hair messy. He smirks at me before offering his arm to walk us to the front door. I scrunch my nose before taking it, regretting this already. I told myself and him just this morning that it was the last time we would be seen together. That it was the last time we hung out.

Now look. Me, Celeste Jones, becoming a "yes man" to Rowan Harper.

We start walking past the people waiting in line to enter the club. I look over my shoulder, confused as to why we are passing the entrance. "Where are we going?"

Rowan tightens his bicep, securing my hand between his ribs and arm. "Don't run."

"Help!" I start screaming, turning my head over my shoulder to get someone's attention. But my body gets thrown into a brick wall. Rowan's face is inches from mine, grinning ear to ear. His scar bunches together as his eyes scan my face.

"Are you kidding me right now?" He laughs and nods to the left of us. I look in the direction to see a large window that shows a dining room filled with people. When I face him again, his smile is gone. "It's a date." He snatches my hand and takes us inside the restaurant. A restaurant I had no idea was even here next to Club Opal.

"Mr. Harper, right this way." The host grabs the menus behind the podium, taking us further into the restaurant. The lights are dim, the round tables covered with white and red tablecloths set with small candles that float in water. We walk through an arched doorway, leaving the main dining room, and are offered a table tucked into a hidden space.

Rowan lets go of my hand to allow me to slide into the booth, his above-average size squeezing in on the opposite side. The host sets down our menus and a waiter instantly replaces him. He tells us the wine of the day, serving us both a glass, and leaves the bottle for us.

"I look crazy," I whisper to him, leaning into the table. "I got dressed for the club, not for dinner." Even though we are deep in the restaurant, not surrounded by anyone, I feel like I have eyes staring at me from all directions. My black dress is too short, my heels too high, and my makeup too much.

"You look beautiful."

I snark, picking up the menu to try and hide the heat rising into my cheeks and ignore the butterflies coming to life in my stomach. "You're lucky I like to eat," I whisper, mainly to myself, but of course he overhears, chuckling from behind his menu.

I scan the menu items, trying to keep my drool behind my lips. A variety of bread is delivered to the table with different kinds of oil to dip into. The waiter speaks in Italian to Rowan, and I set my menu down when Rowan responds back. My mouth slightly parts as I listen, not understanding a word being spoken.

"Grazie," the waiter says, taking both our menus— That one, I understand.

"You speak Italian?"

"I'm half. Mother was from Italy." His hands are intertwined on top of the table, his knuckles bruised and scarred. I take a sip of wine, savoring the sweet acidic burn down my throat. His glance lingers on my hand as I set the glass back down on the table.

"Tell me about her."

He clears his throat, shimmying in the booth. "She was kind. Caring. An avid reader." He looks in his peripheral as a waiter walks by. "She liked to paint."

"Really?"

He nods his head, clearing his throat one more time. "You're from Massachusetts."

"You could say that." I sigh, finishing off my glass of wine and surprised when he tops it off for me. "I was in foster care for my whole life. Started in Massachusetts and hopped from city to city."

"You don't know your birth parents?"

I shake my head, tapping my finger against the glass in my hand to try and distract myself. I don't like pity parties, and with the way he changed the subject from him to me, I assume he's the same way. I also know that if I drink more than one glass of wine, my body will feel relaxed, free, and I start to spew anything that comes to mind. Embarrassing myself in front of Rowan Harper is at the top of my list of things I don't want to do with *Rowan Harper*. Sex currently being number one. But the more he stares at me, his eyes roaming over my features, his tongue darting out every few minutes to lick his lips, and those veins crawling up from his hands to his arms… It's all pushing my number one item lower down the list.

Our waiters politely interrupt us with carts of food. My eyes go wide as different dishes are set in front of us. The waiter tells us to enjoy and leaves us with this feast.

"This is... a lot."

"I wanted you to try everything," he says, opening the napkin that holds my utensils and pushing it toward me.

Number one just flew off the list.

Forty-five minutes later, Rowan and I are sitting next to each other, every plate on the table is one-third gone. An ungodly amount of wine has been consumed between the both of us and I believe the restaurant is closing soon since the music was shut off twenty minutes ago and whispering chatter is no longer coming from the main dining room.

I cover my laugh with my hand, staring at the plates.

"What?" Rowan says, looking at me with a small smile playing on his lips, his eyes squinting with a glossy tint.

"I ate so much food, and I can't even pronounce half of these plates." I point to one of the dishes. "Folye-dela." One of the platters the waiter brought out along with the other desserts.

"Sfogliatella," he repeats, but the correct way, his Italian accent strong as it slips from his tongue.

I moan, throwing my head back. "Why do accents have to be so sexy?"

"You find me sexy?"

I look back at him, moaning again, and put my head back against the booth to try and stop the world from spinning. I can hear Rowan stand, coming to my side, I turn to see him holding out his hand. "Dance with me."

I side-eye him. "No music," I say, just as music turns on. "Are you magic?" He picks up my hand, helping me out of the booth. My legs are like Jell-O, my ankles twisting as I stand on my high heels. Rowan gets on one knee and starts to unbuckle my heels. I place my hands on his shoulders for stability as I step out of the shoes and lose inches of height on him.

One of his arms wraps around my waist while the other holds my hand out to the side of us. We rock back and forth to the music.

"I'd really like to kiss you right now."

My eyes widen. I expected Rowan to be more of an "I want it, I take it" type of guy. And to an extent, he is. To the world he is. But there is this other side of him that he's slowly showing to me— the breakfast date, the feast of a meal he just bought, the slow dancing. I look up at him, his eyes mirroring mine before they point toward my lips. "Then kiss me."

He drops his head, softly pressing his lips against mine. My eyes close and my legs give out. His arm tightens around my waist to keep me upright and I wrap both arms around his neck for stability as his mouth becomes hungrier, devouring my lips with greed, his tongue tapping for entrance. I can feel his bulge growing, hitting my stomach. The kiss goes from a soft, light peck, to something animalistic.

He picks my whole body up with ease, turning me to land on an empty table. He kisses my cheeks, down to my neck. "Once I start, I'm not going to be able to stop." A kiss on my chest, before he leaves one on my breast.

"Then don't." Chills run up my spine as his hands roam up my thighs, bunching my dress at my midriff. He groans when he looks down at my black lace panties, picking up my leg to throw over his shoulder as he plays with the fabric.

"So fucking pretty," he whispers, getting on his knees and dragging me to the end of the table. I look at our surroundings from the end of the hallway to the other that leads to the main dining room.

"Are people here?" I ask in a hushed breath.

"Yes."

I gasp, trying to squirm away, but he shoots his hand down to push me back and rips my panties to the side. "They can't see you." My back arches and my mouth opens when he flicks at my clit with his tongue. He dives his head deeper, bring my hips even closer to the edge as he flattens is tongue and sweeps over my whole pussy, sucking my clit, causing my back to arch off the table. "You taste so fucking good." He removes his mouth and bites the inside of my thigh as if it pains him. He licks the same area, soothing the bite, and uses his finger to tease my entrance.

A fire is building from my toes to up my thighs. I can't help but squeeze his head between my legs when he doesn't let up. A finger pushes past my walls and curls to hit the sweet spot. "Fuck, you're tight." A second finger is added, then a third. My eyes burn with tears as he stretches me beyond my means.

"I need you," I moan.

"You need me, baby?"

I nod my head repeatedly, grabbing at his hair to pull him up.

"Taste how fucking good you are." He drags his tongue along my lips as I reach for his belt, trying to undo the puzzle.

He grabs my wrist, stopping me. "I don't have a condom."

I stare at him, contemplating his distraught face. "Are you clean?"

"Yes."

I squint my eyes and he holds out his pinkie with a whisper of a smile. I interlock my pinkie with his and he lets go of me, unbuckling his belt and bringing his jeans just low enough to free his cock. It bounces out, pre-cum already dripping. I find myself drooling more for that than the food we just ate. He gives me a crooked grin before grabbing my legs to place them on his chest. Pulling his shirt up, holding it with his chin, then looks down as he angles his cock at my entrance.

His head slowly teases and gathers my wetness before he pushes through. My eyes slam shut, my teeth grazing my bottom lip. "It's okay, you can take it, heaven," he says as he kneads his fingers on my thighs.

"Few more inches," he groans.

"There's more?!"

He laughs before he hits my walls, bottoming out. He pulls back out and wastes no time slamming back into me. Our skin echoes in the hallway as it claps together with every stroke. I grip for the edge of the table, trying to hold on, feeling my orgasm crawl to the pit of my stomach. His breath becomes heavier, his strokes turning unwieldy. He picks me up off the table and sits in the booth, placing me on top. I grind until I find my spot. Stars dance in my eyes, and an incoherent noise leaves my mouth. His cock twitches until he's pulling me closer to him and pumping his last few into me.

CHAPTER NINETEEN
ROWAN

"Hello?! Are ye listening to me?!" Jace snaps in my face, trying to get my attention. I close the app I've been staring at for the past few minutes. Celeste is working on a new painting, dancing around her room again. I haven't been able to get her off my mind. Despite the new cases we have, plus my mother's dead-end case—all I can think about is her. "I swear you get a lil' pussy and ye become this obsessive..." Jace mumbles, standing from the couch and putting away his laptop. "Ye call me when you're ready to work again!" He slams my front door closed and I pick up my phone once more, staring at the video. I zoom in closer to see something off. She's doing the same move repeatedly before the camera goes dark.

Three knocks hit my door, and I look toward the sound before looking back at my black phone screen. Snickering, I throw the device onto the other couch. I swing the door open, assuming it's Jace, but look down a few inches to see Celeste standing in the doorway.

"Hide the cameras better." She smirks and pushes past me to enter the house. She throws herself onto the couch and I can't help but gawk at her.

She sits straight up, eyes bulging, and her palm hits her forehead. "Oh god, I'm so sorry. I'm stupid. I got bored. Lily is at work, and I figured I could come here—"

I close my front door and sit in the seat next to her. "Tell me about the painting you're working on."

Her eyes flutter and her brows crease. Biting her bottom lip, she folds her legs underneath her and tucks her hair behind her ears. "It's regarding the war that's happening in another country." She chews on her cheek and looks around the house. "And someone keeps buying all my original paintings—"

I look at my office door, making sure it's closed.

"Which is great. Even my prints are being sold. Lots of donating happening. But my boss keeps texting me about where I can find work and all I can think about is finishing my stories on canvases."

"You're free now, let's go do one."

Her eyebrow perks. "Rowan Harper wants to be paparazzi with me?"

I shrug my shoulder.

"*The* Rowan Harper!"

"Is that supposed to mean something?" I wait for her to respond but she stares at me with a flat face and blinks repeatedly.

Curling her lips, she says, "Fuck it. I have my camera in the car."

I fucked up bad. Celeste and I are sitting outside a restaurant as she secretly takes out her camera and places it on the table facing behind us. Behind us toward Brittany McLauren. I have my hoodie placed over my head, hunched into the table like a damn fool.

"You can relax, nobody is going to notice you." Celeste giggles and I opt to pull my hoodie even further over my face. I know she's right. Nobody will see me, it's half past eight. The only lights outside are the dim string lights hanging from the cabana. We took the furthest table in the corner and Brittany and her latest potential husband-victim are in the center of the patio.

Celeste presses the button on her camera and it flickers a bright light, the camera shuttering as it takes the photo. I look up at her as she stares at me with wide eyes.

"Hey!"

I shove my seat from under me, Celeste grabbing her bag as I snatch her hand and we run inside the restaurant. Celeste giggles as I pull her out and we both dash to her car. When we jump in, we notice a security guard chasing us from the restaurant.

"Go, go!" I tell her, slamming my hands on the dashboard. Celeste screeches into traffic, nearly causing a collision as her old Chevy fishtails.

"The fuck did you do to this car?" I hold onto the "oh shit" handle, praying that this is not how I die. I deserve a better ending than my girl driving worse than Jace through New York.

"A turbo kit," she sing-songs. "And an exhaust. Possibly some illegal tuning." She shrugs and my hold tightens on the handle as she jumps a curve, making a left turn at the next light. A "whoopsie," leaves her mouth with another giggle.

"Pull over, I'm driving."

"Hell no."

I look at her and she scrunches her nose at me. "You drive foreign. I drive American muscle. You wouldn't know how to handle my baby."

"I don't think *you* know how to handle this baby."

She pffts, waving me off, and slows the vehicle down. "I'd never do anything to destroy my car. I worked my ass off for this." Her hand pats at the steering wheel. "When I was a kid, I knew as soon as I could afford a car, I could get out of the system. Found ole' Selena here—"

"You named your car?"

Her head swivels to me and then back to the road. "Of course! I found her being sold, broken down to bits. Every paycheck I had went to her. Once I got her running, I took off. Lived in her for three months once I got to New York. Then met Lily and everything became history."

"Old Selena here doesn't even have Bluetooth."

She wags her finger at me and presses the button on her radio. She digs into her compartment until she finds a CD. "Ever seen one of these?" She twirls the iridescent circle in the air and laughs. "Save Your Tears" by Milky Chance plays through the speakers and she sings along to every verse.

Once the song is over, she turns down the music and looks toward me. "So, Brittany?"

I swallow the heavy saliva that gets stuck in my throat. "You know her?"

"Of course. She's a McLauren. Her father owns a couple of banks, and her mother has her own makeup line. She also seems to be your girlfriend." Celeste looks back and forth from me to the street.

"And what gave you that impression?" My grip tightens on the handle. How the fuck and who the fuck told her that? Me and Brittany were years ago and never went public.

"Caught a little photo of her trying to fuck you the night you came inside me." The streetlights pass over her face, showing one of her eyebrows raised.

Her calm tone could be intimidating to anyone, maybe me included. But you know who is not intimidating? Fucking Lily. "Lily can get fired for taking a photo."

"And I can open my car door and push you into oncoming traffic." Her finger presses the unlock button. "We may not be anything, Rowan Harper, but you've made a fool out of me once all because a paparazzi caught us in a coffee shop. If she is your girlfriend, you tell me now."

"So that's why you brought me along?"

"You offered to come."

We're silent in the car as we come to a red light and Celeste unbuckles her seat belt. A smile tips my lips knowing she truly might push me out of her car. Since I'd like to not be run over by traffic and because I despise Brittany McLauren, I tell her, "My father wanted me to marry Brittany, have an arranged marriage between our families. If you still have the photo, zoom into my face and you can see the disgust. I would rather swallow a million thumb tacks than be in a relationship with that woman. She came into the club asking for Jace and my assistance to conduct a private investigation on her new man back there to see if the money he says he has is real," I spit it out quickly since halfway through my explanation, she unbuckles my seat belt.

Celeste buckles herself back in when the light turns green and proceeds through the intersection.

I re-clasp mine. "And because I fucking hate her and the fact that she thought seducing me would make me say yes. I kicked her to the curb, but obviously your friend didn't catch or tell you that part."

She hums, tapping her finger against the steering wheel before turning her music back on. We listen to her playlist—Milkey Chance, Billie Eilish, Sia, and The Teskey Brothers—all the way back to my house. The back of my neck beads with sweat as the car idles in my driveway, neither of us saying a word.

My stomach feels like it's leaking acid as I wait for her to say something. I refuse to allow this to be the end of us. I can't allow it. Won't allow it. "Come inside," I tell her.

She angles her body toward me. "You know, you're really demanding."

I blink at her with my stony face until she starts smiling and I become intoxicated. I typically don't smile. For anyone. About anything. But for her— With her, I find myself smiling significantly more.

She turns her car off and I follow her up my porch. As soon as I close the door, I grab her arm and whip her around. I slam my lips on hers, begging for another taste. This time, she doesn't wait. She hops in the air, wrapping her legs around my waist, and if I believed in a god, I'd thank them. I take us down to the couch. Her hands slide underneath my sweater and I help her rip it off me. Her hands are already reaching for my zipper as I hurriedly rip her shirt above her head.

No bra.

Thank a god.

I grab a handful of her breast and suck on the tan nipple like it's my last meal. A delicious treat sent from the above just for me. Her moans sound like little angels whispering in my ear until I bite at her nipple, tugging it between my teeth, and those moans turn into whimpers. "You feel good."

"You're not even inside me yet."

I work my way to the next breast. "I don't need to be. You feel like home." Her nails stop grazing my back and I internally shoot myself for saying something like that. I bite her nipple again to try and distract her, her nails creating indents in my skin and I continue licking around her body.

Biggest Fan

It wasn't a lie. Celeste gives me comfort. Comfort I haven't had in years. And I'd do anything and everything to make sure it stays that way.

She slips from underneath me and I back away to look down, finding her on her knees. She rips my pants down and grabs my cock with a hard squeeze. I fall back on my coffee table, hearing a crack from the glass underneath.

Her tongue darts out, starting at the base of my cock, and works its way to my head, twirling the tip of her tongue on my slit. I nearly cum from the sight of her hand gliding up and down as she drools on me. My mind feels like it's going to explode from the pressure, forcing me to grab ahold of the table instead of her hair.

Until she swallows me whole.

I grunt and buck my hips up to go deeper, the warmth and wetness behind her lips. Her eyes shut as she opens her throat to take all of me. "Fuck, Celeste."

My hand reaches out and I grab ahold of her scalp. Her breasts swinging, tears falling from her eyes, ass perched in the air while she is on all fours… I fucking wish I had more hands to explore her body while her mouth bobs on my cock.

My eyes roll back and I moan when her fingers start kneading at my balls.

This woman wants to fucking kill me.

I feel the buildup, my dick twitching when she hollows her cheeks and her tongue lingers at my head. Her hold tightens around my base as she strokes me off until I'm coming deep down her throat. What fucking does it for me is when she moans as she swallows me dry.

She leans back, using her fingers to wipe at the side of her lips.

Just as I am about to pick her up and take her to my room to finish this, my house is drenched in red light.

CHAPTER TWENTY
ROWAN

"What's going on?" Celeste wraps her arms around her breasts as I stand up, quickly buttoning my jeans. I throw her my jacket and run for the foyer table, grabbing my pistol and making sure it's loaded.

"Rowan?!" I push Celeste toward my office, entering my code and taking her inside. "Rowan?" Her voice turns to a whisper as she looks at my office walls. My walls that are covered with all her original paintings.

Well, too late to explain now.

I start opening my file cabinets, looking for my screwdriver. Celeste stands in the middle of my room doing a complete three-sixty. Once I find the screwdriver, I shove the head into a gap underneath my desk, popping off the secret compartment. I grab the Glock, checking for bullets, and slam it on my desk.

"You have so much explaining to do." She walks to the right wall and points to her old prints from three years ago. I gather her and drag her toward my desk and point underneath.

She looks at the small space, then at me. "I can't."

I shake my head, knowing we have less than thirty seconds, my silent alarm still blinking red. "I'm so sorry." I hand her one of the guns and push her shoulders down until she crawls underneath into the space. "Do not come out until I come get you."

"Rowan, please tell me what's going on."

Fucking timing of these people is impeccable. I kiss her forehead and open up another drawer, pulling out my silencer to the barrel. I look at Celeste one more time. She sits holding her knees to her chest, her body shaking beneath my black jacket. Her curls are wild, messy, and her eyes glossy and red. I wish there was another way.

I peek my head over the desk, hearing the front door open. I stand and run to turn off the lights. Hard footsteps echo through the living room and ascend the stairs. Once they are all above me, I run back to Celeste, extending my pinkie to her. "Promise you won't come out until someone comes and gets you."

"Someone?!" she whispers. "It better be you." She stares at my pinkie longer and sweat drips at the nape of my neck. When she finally locks her pinkie with mine, I kiss our hands and leave her there.

Biggest Fan

I quietly close the door behind me and run to my garage. Holding the door open and stretching to reach the breaker, I shut off all the power in the house.

Time to party.

I close the garage door and hear them mumbling upstairs. Only one flashlight is on, scanning the bottom of my stairs. I wait in the dark underneath, hearing boots slam their way down to the first floor. Two of them descend the stairs with their automatic rifles pointed. They turn left, heading to my kitchen, and I silently follow.

Splitting up, one near my sink, the other near my dining table, I take the one in my kitchen and hit him in the back of his head with the end of my gun. In the corner of my eye, a silver reflection is flowing my way. It enters my shoulder, and I grunt. Turning around, I raise my gun, firing at his friend before he can even touch the trigger. I point to the man at my feet and send another bullet. My shoulder aches as I reach behind me, grabbing ahold of the knife lodged in my skin, and rip it out. It clinks onto the floor next to the dead body.

More footsteps come from upstairs. I hide behind the half-wall, counting his steps until I know he's about to hit the living room. I emerge from around the corner, shooting his knee and finishing him off between the eyes.

Three more and I have no more time to play. I run for the stairs, finding all three dummies huddled in a circle. My finger pulls the trigger three more times before they even have the chance to fully turn around.

Once they all drop like flies, I search their bodies for any explosives, any phones, anything that can tell me who they are.

When I come up empty-handed, I scratch my head with the barrel of the gun and make my way to the garage. I hit the switches, turning on the lights for inside the house and my strobe light for outside.

If my silent alarm went off, that means someone is in a trap.

I walk out my front door, hearing the whimpers. My strobe light points directly into the small forest of trees. I follow the sound until I see a man in a balaclava, grabbing ahold of his leg that is clamped in the bear trap. His bone protrudes from his shin, blood clotting with the fallen leaves.

Celeste was lucky she missed this one.

"Who are you?" I ask.

He spits toward me, trying to tear his leg out.

Interesting.

I lean against a tree, watching to see if he would prefer losing a leg than tell me who they are. His teeth grind against each other the harder he pulls. His friends left him to die. Took his gun and left him to rot.

A cracking sound erupts from the trap, and he screams into the night. I raise my gun and send a bullet. He tumbles sideways when the bullet connects. No need for the neighbors to call the cops because they hear screaming.

I pull off his mask to see nobody recognizable. "Fuck." I sigh, throwing the mask onto the ground and making my way back to the house.

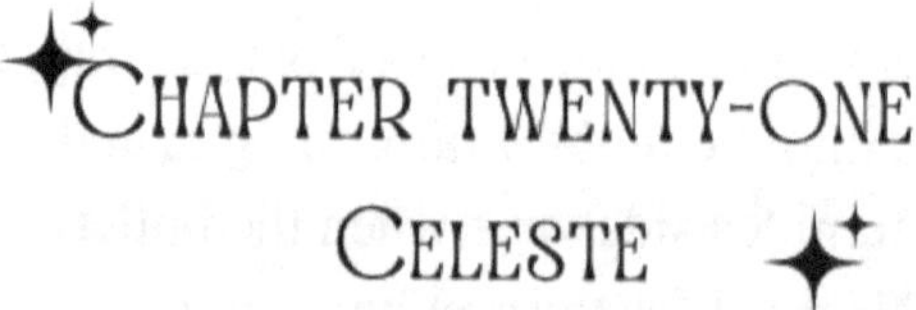

CHAPTER TWENTY-ONE
CELESTE

My hands cover my ears, blocking them from the sound of multiple gunshots. The weapon taps at my temple as I shake. I don't know what Rowan was thinking giving me this gun. I have no idea how to use it, and I don't want to use it. Tears stream down my face and I start rocking back and forth.

I scream when something grabs my shoulder, and chuck the weapon out into the open.

"You're supposed to pull the trigger, not throw it." Rowan grabs my hand, pulling me from underneath the desk. Once standing, I immediately drop my head into my hands and start crying uncontrollably. He pulls me into his chest, shushing me. "You're okay. It's okay." His hands rub my back as I hiccup and sob into his skin.

Once I am able to catch my breath, I push him away. "What the fuck?!" I rub my nose with the back of my hand. "What just happened?! Is this a joke?"

"If I knew, I'd tell you... Maybe. Just stay right here, we need to leave."

I stare at him in shock as he hurries out the door and my eyes search the ceiling, listening to his fast footsteps above me. I can hear what sounds like drawers being slammed closed, and large thumps hitting the ground. Within minutes, he is standing back in front of me, dropping large duffle bags at my feet. "What are you doing?"

"I am getting us out of here." He grabs his phone from his desk and immediately starts typing.

"Where are we going? I can't leave! I have work and—"

"You mean the job you just told me a few hours ago you don't even want to do?" He grabs my face with both of his hands. "Celeste, whoever was here to kill me, saw your car outside. High chance they took a photo of your license plate. Or they followed us here. They could know who you are, and I am not letting you out of my sight until I figure out who *they* are."

I try to swallow the lump in my throat. "They're going to kill me?" I whisper. My heart is beating so fast it could rip a hole in my chest. My head is throbbing from crying, and I still can't stop shaking.

"Nobody is killing you." He places a kiss on my forehead and turns around, putting his phone to his ear.

"See, this is why I didn't want to get involved with you." I start pacing around his office, talking *mainly* to myself. "First, it was the magazine. Now you have people hunting us and you don't know *who* or *why*." I shuffle my feet on his rug and look up to see him standing in front of me, his phone still to his ears with narrow eyes.

"Fuck!" He brings the phone down, turning around, and calls someone else. He turns his back on me, and I notice the blood running down over his tattoos.

"Rowan you're hurt." My hand reaches out to touch him.

He shrugs away. "I'm fine. I need to get you out of here." He puts his phone down, scrolling and dialing another number.

There is a deep gash, too close to his spine for my liking. A few more inches and he could have been paralyzed. Does he not feel this? I look around the office. There has to be something to dress this, close the wound, stop the bleeding. Something. I open all the drawers of his desk, finding most of them empty except for the last one—a set of keys, and I know exactly what they open.

I hear him call my name as I walk out of the office and into the living room. I stop when something drips right in front of me, looking down to find a pool of blood staining his marble floors. When I look up, bodies are hanging from the top floor, their arms suspended between the balusters.

Biggest Fan

I slap my hand over my mouth to cover my whimper, looking left to see another lifeless body near his couch. I run toward the hallway underneath the stairs and shuffle the keys in my hand, trying to find the one for this door.

When I'm finally able to unlock all the deadbolts, I open the door only to have an alarm go off. I stare at the door handle, not realizing a code was needed along with the keys. The alarm is quickly shut off. I turn behind me to see the empty hallway and dash down the steep steps, my hands grazing the wall in search of a light switch. Bright lights fill the space, and my eyes widen when I see large hooks swinging from the concrete ceiling. A pair of chains is deadbolted into the ground. Tools, guns, weapons all locked behind metal bars on the wall.

I hit the last step, my feet sending chills up my thighs from the cold concrete floor. Darks stains are splattered near my feet and I whisper, "Private investigator my ass." I run to a storage cabinet and find a white medical kit: sterile suture threads, needles, blades, and multiple scissor-like tools. I doubt I will need all of this, but I take the whole kit and turn the light off behind me.

Exiting the hallway, I turn into his kitchen, keeping my eyes forward and stepping wide to avoid more bodies. As long as I don't look down, I won't throw up. I open his glass-wall kitchen storage that shows off his luxurious alcohol collection. Grabbing a clear bottle I assume is vodka and another bottle of brown liquid with a name I refuse to pronounce, I run back to his office carrying everything in my arms.

Rowan stands in the corner, staring at what's in my hands with his phone to his ear. "What are you doing?" he asks, his lips folding down.

I nod toward the couch. "Sit."

"We don't have time."

"Rowan Harper. Sit your ass down."

He scrunches his eyes at me. "You're pale. I tried to stop you from going out there." He hangs up the phone and sits down on his leather couch. I follow, sitting behind him and placing the medical kit on my lap.

"Who were you trying to call?" I ask to try and distract him, or maybe myself. It's been years since I had to suture someone up.

"John."

I hand him the clear liquor bottle, giving him time to open the cap and take two large gulps. He hands it back to me and I pour the liquid over my hands, straight onto his nice wood flooring.

"That bottle is more expensive than your car, Celeste," he says through gritted teeth, looking at the new puddle on his floor.

"Good. Then my hands should be sterile." I bring the bottle to my lips, taking a swig as well. I choke on the dry taste, regretting the shot. Who the hell spends this much money on something that tastes exactly like rubbing alcohol? I pour some over his gash and can see his jaw tense. I hand him the other bottle for the pain.

"Do you know what you're doing?" He peeks over his shoulder, but I ignore him as I focus on pulling the thread through the needle and tying it.

I pinch his skin together and our eyes meet. "You ready?" He nods his head and takes another shot. The needle punctures his skin. "One of the families I lived with used to do things to some of the older children. That's when I learned." I keep my breath steady as I make the second suture.

"Did they touch you?" Rowan practically growls and I have to pause to make sure it's still him. My stomach drops and my eyes catch his knuckles turning white against the handle of the bottle.

"No." I focus back on my task. "I wasn't old enough. Seven at the time. They figured they could get away with the older children. The parents would say it was self-defense, that the kids started it." This would be a lot easier if he wasn't all muscle. My fingers are starting to ache from keeping his skin together while I force the needle through the non-existent flesh on his back.

He grunts when I push the needle too deep. I bite my tongue, silently apologizing. "Did you keep in contact with anyone you grew up with? Any of the other kids?" he asks.

"No. I tried to leave the past behind me. Although there was another girl, at one point. Sasha. I'd love to know where she is, how her life turned out." I smile to myself, remembering all the good times Sasha and I had when things weren't so dark. We were housed with two other boys and our favorite thing to do was tease them and force them to play dress-up with us. I was transferred out of the house, and on the last day of us being together, we cried and pled for them not to separate us.

I finish the last stitch and tie the end. "All done."

Rowan turns toward me. "Thank you." His phone lights up between us, breaking our contact. "Okay, let's go." He shoots up, grabbing the duffle bags.

"Wait!" I hold out my hand to stop him from leaving his office. "What about Lily? I can't leave her by herself. And I have no clothes. Where are we even going? What about my job and—"

"I sent Jace to look after Lily. I have clothes being delivered and Jace is going to email your boss that you quit."

My mouth drops open. "He quit my job?!"

CHAPTER TWENTY-TWO
ROWAN

It took less than twenty minutes on my motorcycle to get us to my private jet. I refused Celeste a chance to breathe after I told her she quit her job. I saw the panic start to rise in her face, so I had to drag her to the garage, secure a helmet on her head, throw the duffle bags over my shoulder, and place her pretty ass on my bike. She doesn't need to be paparazzi anymore. I take care of her now. No matter what it is. But I didn't want her to find out that I was the one buying her artwork just yet.

But here we are.

The whole ride to the jet, all I could think about was how Celeste grew up, seeing the abuse other children endured. Imaging her going through any abuse herself makes me want to commit mass murder. If I find out she lied to me, and that she was the one having to stitch herself up… I cannot promise any friendly outcome for anyone who laid their hands on her. She stated she wants to leave her past behind. Unlike me. I can't. I can't leave my past behind because I'm still searching for it.

Celeste walks past me once we enter the plane and takes a seat a full row behind me. We have a long, ten-hour flight to Italy, and I refuse to be on a plane with a grumpy brat. I get up and sit in the chair right in front of her. She pretends to ignore me, staring out the small window with her head in her hand. "Would you like to know where we are going now?"

She rolls her eyes and tsks at me. "Does it matter? You seem to have everything already planned."

"Is that an issue? My apologies for taking care of you."

Her lip twitches and she whips her neck to look at me, fury permeating her eyes. "I never asked to be taken care of. I never asked for any of this." She waves her hands in the air. "I didn't want to be involved with you because I knew there would be drama. But this." Again, she waves her hands in the air before she claps them together. "This is worse than drama. I have people out there who probably want to kill me, all because I fucked you?"

I can't help but smile, biting the inside of my cheek to stop myself from laughing. "It was a good fuck though."

"Ugh. You're intolerable."

"I think you can take it." I shrug my shoulder and she crinkles her nose, only making my smile grow. But when my heart starts pounding and the large inhale I take doesn't make it stop, and my stomach feels like it wants to cut through my skin and deplete all my stomach acid, I realize I have to say, "I'm sorry." Her face flattens and she falls further into the seat. "I know none of this is what you want. Or what you may expect. I know you probably want nothing to do with me, but I couldn't—can't—get you out of my head since that first day we met."

"Yeah, very memorable, by the way," she says and sucks in her lips.

I know she is being sarcastic, but I feel the need to tell her everything. Tell her the truth. I wait a second, watching her as she tries to avoid eye contact. "This isn't something I'd ever want to involve you in. My personal life. But goddammit, Celeste Jones, you are something else. Special, good in the heart. I've only had one good person in my life who was full of love, and I lost her. So, when I met you, I knew you were full of it and I have been trying everything to hold on, to steal, to keep it for myself. It has been selfish of me and my actions have consequences. So, I promise, once this is all over and done, I will leave you alone. You can go back to your daily life and I won't interfere." A part of me cracks and shatters, still feeling sick to my stomach and hating the way all of that spilled from my tongue. I'm not sure I can hold on to that promise, but I make it anyway. A piece of me will die every fucking day not seeing her, but if she agrees, I'll give her want she wants.

I'd give her the world. The moon. The stars. The heavens. And I'd close the doors to hell. All for her.

She blinks at me repeatedly. I can see her mind processing everything. She looks down at her hands intertwined in her lap. Sweat drips down the nape of my neck as I wait for her to say something. I wish she would say something.

"Where are we going?"

Not what I wanted her to say… "Italy."

Chapter Twenty-Three
Celeste

I'm woken up by Rowan letting me know we've arrived. As we walk down the stairs of the jet, I thank our pilot, who looks less like a pilot and more like a hitman, and I may have whispered a quick little "thank you" to the universe as well. A part of me feels bad for chewing Rowan out. Once he told me we were coming to Italy, he got out of his seat, disappeared to the back of the plane, and never came back out. I wasn't lying when I said I didn't want any of this, but I feel like I'm on the edge of a cliff with Rowan. There is a part of me that wants more of him. A part of me that wants to help him. Help him find his mom. Give him the home he so desperately craves. He carries this dark cloud over his head and only lets the sun shine when I'm around him.

I can see it. Feel it.

He's a good man who's been handed the blade side of the knife. He may do some questionable things, but he does them for all the right reasons.

Rowan helps me down the stairs and opens the door to an all-black SUV. The windows are tinted so dark that I can see my full reflection. I look like I just crawled from the depths of hell. My curls are wild, knotted, in a messy bun. Dark circles have completely invaded the space under my eyes, and I am still in the same jacket Rowan gave me last night.

Last night.

A slight hint of his taste still lingers on my lips. Everything was great before it all went to shit. I never thought I would walk up to Rowan Harper's house and be civil. Let alone do the very X-rated things I did to him. Rowan said that he would leave me alone after this is all over, but I don't think I want him to leave me alone.

I don't think *I* want to leave *him* alone.

"We will be staying at my cottage on Lake Garda," he says, typing away on his phone.

Our view currently consists of a beach and multiple buildings beside it, but none of them are cottage-like. "Are we close?"

"Twenty-minutes away. We are currently in Montichiari." There's that beautiful accent again. He finally looks up from his phone and gives me a tight-lipped smile and my heart crumbles. I hurt him. I know I did. I hurt him when I didn't respond to his confession.

Biggest Fan

Rowan Harper, the most handsome bachelor in all of New York, can't get his mind off me, and I didn't return any type of sentiment.

But that is one of the main things on the long list of what is wrong with me: being able to express my feelings. Feelings, communication of feelings, giving affection. My emotions are either at one end of the spectrum or the other, never able to find middle ground. Sometimes affection makes my skin crawl. Like my soul leaves my body from the discomfort. Not all the time, but most of the time. It's a constant battle in my own mind.

Just like my feelings with Rowan Harper.

We have a silent drive as I stare out the window, viewing all the new architecture, and when the driver slows down, pulling to the side, Rowan says, "Welcome to Largo Di Garda." He exits the vehicle and opens my door. I stare down the hill engraved with stone steps that take you down to the property. A two-story building is surrounded by the greenest grass I've ever seen and sits on top of a cliff that overlooks the lake. At the lake's center is a singular mountain.

I rush down the stairs like a child on Christmas morning. Kicking off my shoes, I race through the grass until I'm standing on a brick wall that outlines the cliff, a twenty-plus foot drop down into the waters below. I close my eyes, soaking in the beating sun and breathing the fresh air.

This might be worth almost dying for.

I can feel Rowan's presence behind me and the smell of a… cigarette? I turn around to see the cherry-red tip hanging from his lips. "Can I not enjoy my first time breathing fresh air since living in New York? You had to light a cigarette to ruin it?" He takes a long drag before flicking it into the distance. He places his hands in his pockets and studies the view in front of us.

"So, you're enjoying yourself?" He bites the inner corner of his cheek, highlighting his sharp jawline.

"We just arrived. I can't make statements yet." I grab my shoes and head toward the house. A two-story white brick building. Six windows with actual shutters—that probably open, as opposed to the ones in New York that stay nailed shut—adorn each side. Above is a red rooftop with a balcony, and out front is a small porch with lawn chairs, a small grill, and multiple potted plants surrounding it. A fucking cottage my ass. This is a house. A mini mansion.

I open the side door and my mouth drops. The first view is the kitchen. The cabinets are painted blue-ish green, a bronze lamp hanging from the ceiling above an eight-seater table. Pots and pans that are probably worth more than my rent hang above the kitchen island. An arch leads to the living room, which is decorated with huge paintings and two leather couches on the sides of a large brick fireplace. A brick staircase leads upstairs. "This is all yours?" I ask, spinning on my feet while looking at the tall ceilings.

"Yes, but I don't come here often," Rowan says, leaning against the archway. He disappears into the kitchen, and I walk up to one of the paintings hanging on the wall. Its technique is similar to one I saw hanging in his office, one that I knew wasn't mine. It's an abstract oil painting. All of my work is abstract, but oil paintings are something I tend to avoid. Being able to reveal colors, create depth and contrast, and wait for the paint to dry all requires the patience I don't have.

"My mother's work."

I turn around, almost tripping over my own feet to find Rowan standing behind me with two glasses of red wine.

"I used to watch her paint in her office all the time. Then one day, she just stopped. I remember hearing her and my father fight over a painting, but I was a kid and didn't understand. Until one day, a bunch of people came to our house and took all the paintings she had done away." He hands me a glass and sits on the couch, still staring at the painting. "I jumped into the back of the truck where they were storing all her work." The side of his mouth curls up before he takes a sip of his wine. "I stole as many as I could before they left."

I take a sip of the wine, humming when the fresh liquor pours down my throat. "How old were you?"

"Nine."

"Did you ever find any of the other paintings?"

"No." He scowls, taking another sip, and turns to look at the largest painting on his wall. I follow his eyes to a canvas of a tree covered in moss, sitting in the middle of the lake.

Her paintings meant something to him at that age, and he lost them. Years later, he lost her. I wish there was more I could say to him, something that would make him feel better. But I never knew who my parents were, so I'll never truly understand the loss. The closest I got was Sasha, but I doubt she even remembers who I am, let alone the things we went through or the feelings we shared.

"I will show you to your room so you can get cleaned up."

I follow him upstairs to a square landing, two doors on each side of the hallway. I peek inside each one we pass. A bathroom, an office, and two bedrooms across from each other. He leans against one bedroom doorframe, scratching his neck before pointing to the bedroom behind me. I turn to see my luggage already on the bed.

"When I sent Jace to watch over Lily, I told him to have her pack some clothes for you. When you're finished, meet me downstairs." He leaves the doorframe, *leaves me*, and walks down the stairs.

Lily packing for me has to be the worse idea to ever exist. I open my suitcase to find multiple pairs of lingerie, dresses, shorts, and blouses. Nothing even close to being comfortable to wear.

Great.

I grab the closest dress that won't squeeze my tits or highlight my ass and head toward the bathroom. I let the warm water run down my body as I slam my face into my hands. Maybe I can blame this all on Lily. I was blowing up her phone while she was at work because I was bored and I was confessing my hatred for Rowan after seeing the photo of him and Brittany. Her only short, multiple text messages to me were:

"Your room stinks."

"You need to get out of the house."

"If you're thinking about him this much, just go and kiss and make up."

"Leave me alone, my phone feels like a vibrator on my boobs."

I was pissed when I got home and saw Lily texted me a photo. Right after he filled me with delicious Italian food and fucked me raw on the table, Rowan goes back to the club to have Barbie Brittany's tits in his face? It made me jealous, even though we weren't serious—aren't serious, and I still don't know how I feel about him.

Did I believe his story? Unfortunately, yes. Now that I know Rowan, I can't see him being with someone like Brittany. Did my hormones get the best of me when he told me to come inside? Again, yes. Then everything went sideways with the whole "We have people trying to get inside the house so I'm going to shove you under my desk and kill them all."

So, I guess the real blame should be put on me. For not knowing my feelings for Rowan Harper.

After the much-needed shower, and shower thoughts, I throw on the dress, comb out my curls, and put on some concealer to hide these dark circles. I apply my lipgloss and head out of the bedroom. Stopping on the third step on the stairs, I lift my head up and look down over the railing.

Is something on fire?

✦Chapter Twenty-Four
Celeste ✦

I run down the rest of the stairs and through the living room, stopping at the archway to see Rowan on the porch, his back toward me. He's standing in front of the grill flipping what looks to be meat.

On fire.

I slowly walk to the glass sliding door and stop when Rowan turns to look at me with scrunched eyes, the charcoal meat between a set of tongs. "I hope you like it fucking well done." He shakes his head, throwing the meat on a plate.

I can't help but laugh and he turns to me, scowling. I step outside, taking the tongs from his hand, and grab both pieces of the charred meat before walking toward the lake and chucking them in the distance. Rowan stares at me with slightly parted lips and as I walk past him, I place my hand on his shoulder and say, "It's okay. You tried." I continue my way into the kitchen and rifle through the cabinets until I find a bag of rice and tortillas. In the fridge I find some more steak and vegetables.

"Everything is so kept up for you to not come here very often," I say as I check the expiration dates on all the items. I turn around to find Rowan right behind me, looking at me—and if I am deciphering his emotions correctly—with compassion? Whatever look he is giving me right now makes me curl my toes and quickly look away.

"I have someone who comes and checks in on the house."

I give him a nod and try to reach for one of the hanging pans. Rowan steps behind me, placing his hand on my hip, and reaches above me to bring it down. He places it on the stove and walks toward the dining room table to sit.

After twenty minutes of silence, I turn around, seeing him on his laptop. I open my mouth, then quickly close it, not wanting to disrupt his work. I focus on the meal prep in front of me, cutting up the fresh cilantro, tomatoes, onions, and jalapenos. But a question has been eating at me ever since I stepped foot in his office.

"What's wrong, heaven?"

I set the knife down. This nickname he gave me the first time we met. It makes the blood rush straight to my heart anytime he uses it. When I look up, his eyes haven't left the computer screen. "Why did you buy my paintings?"

He finally disregards his screen and gives me a wide smile, stretching his scar. A scar he has never shown to the world, one he never talks about, but it doesn't bother me. It's not ugly, it doesn't affect how handsome he already is. If anything, it only makes him more handsome. It gives him this bad-ass edgy look that I know most girls would fawn over, but for whatever reason, he doesn't bring it up, he doesn't show or tell anyone about it.

"Because I'm your biggest fan." He leans back in his chair, crossing his arms and giving me a slight grin. For a second, I lose my train of thought as I stare at his bulging biceps. But I shake my head to ignore the fantasy that is about to erupt in my mind.

I pick the knife up and resume cutting. "You know, I really thought I was finally getting somewhere with my art. My paintings were selling, even my older ones. But no, it was just my obsessive stalker, and now kidnapper, who bought them all." I can feel stinging behind my eyes and I'm blaming it on the onions.

Rowan scrapes his chair back and comes to stand at my side. I put the knife back down and turn, leaning my hip into the kitchen island.

His deep-set eyes stare down at me. "First of all, I am obsessed with you, if I didn't make that clear enough on the plane. Second, you stalked me first. And third…" He lifts my chin with his index finger. "Your work deserves to be in a showroom. Your work deserves and will receive the recognition. You deserve everything this life has to offer and more, and I am going to make sure you receive it all." Our breaths collide as we lock eyes.

"What if I don't want your help?" I ask with a hushed tone.

"Not sure I can give you that option." His hand roams my lower back until he reaches the nape of my neck. I bite my bottom lip when his thumb rubs along my pulse. When his grip tightens along my neck, bringing our faces closer I decide, to close the distance. Our lips collide and he instantly gets greedy, pushing my back into the kitchen island. His hands wrap around my thighs and he picks me up. He shoves the cutting board aside, making room to settle me on top of the counter while his tongue dances with mine.

Our breaths could be heard from two towns over as we scramble to remove his shirt and push my dress over my hips. With Rowan, everything is so quick and easy. I can be completely angry at him for bringing me into this whirlwind of drama and all he has to do is place his lips on mine and everything else disappears.

Once Rowan's eyes wander to my open skin, he falls to his knees, his fingers tensing against my thighs. "No panties today?" He slowly rubs my swollen clit with his thumb. My head falls back with a moan and my hips buck, needing more.

My body is begging for him to be inside of me. I can feel my own cum dripping. My legs tensing. My toes curling. And in this moment, I don't care what my mind thinks. I throw it away like a bad picture, and when he groans, grabbing my breast—kneading it forcefully and says, "Fuck, you're so beautiful"—I pretend that I don't feel my own heart melt inside my chest.

He quickens his pace faster on my clit. "I want you to come all over this counter. Can you do that for me, baby?" he asks, leaving kisses on the inside of my thighs, and I nod my head immediately, using my heels to pull him closer. I moan faintly when I feel his warm mouth inhale my clit.

He spreads me wider, the sound of my ass squeaking on the counter as he pulls my legs closer to the edge. I feel his tongue go from the entrance, back up, flicking at my nerve, then making his way around. Exploring me like he hasn't been here before. My legs vibrate when he moans into my skin, and I squeeze my thighs against his cheeks as my cries of ecstasy penetrate the air.

From his tongue to his finger, he teases my entrance, causing tingles to shoot from my feet to my lower stomach. I try to make every second count, but when my organs squeeze tight, I know I'm not able to hold on any longer. I put a foot on each of his shoulders, grabbing the back of his head for stability as I ride his face.

My body shakes with force until my feet fall off his shoulders and I slump down, resting my back across the kitchen counter. I don't catch my breath when he scoops me up and carries me into the living room. His lips press kisses along my neck as he lays me down on floor with his hands on either side of my head.

"I want your cum all over this house." His fingers slide back down between my thighs, gathering my wetness, and swiping it down his tongue. It's an erotic scene I would like to have engraved in my brain for the rest of my life: his two fingers against his tongue, his dark hair splayed on his forehead with his eyes only on me. All for me.

I reach down to his jeans, undoing his button. The sight of his dick makes the hairs on the back of my neck stand. Beautifully proportioned, throbbing veins, and pre-cum already dripping. He leans onto his elbow and uses his other hand to rub his cock up and down before thrusting into me in one motion. He stills, leaving it inside of me, both of us holding our breaths, before he slowly starts thrusting in and out.

I may have blacked out a few times. After the living room, he took me to the shower to clean up, but decided he wasn't finished. Now the shower curtain and rod in his en-suite lie on the floor. Then, while I was getting changed, he told me my body was too perfect to cover up. Now we both lie on his bed, out of breath, staring at the ceiling.

"You don't like deadbolts or small spaces."

I look toward Rowan to see him staring down at me. "You don't like deadbolts or small spaces," he repeats.

"Okay, Captain Obvious. Thanks for the palm read."

"Have you talked to anyone about it?" He sits up and rakes his hands into my curls, using his fingertips to massage my scalp.

"What, like a therapist?" I laugh.

"I'm serious, Celeste." His fingers stop, resulting in my eyebrows scrunching together. "I can get you one."

"I think you've done enough." I try to slide off the bed, but he stops me.

"I don't think I have done enough." He pulls me into his side and lays my head across his chest. I think the world would flip upside down if they knew how soft and caring Rowan Harper really is. "Tell me about it."

I take a deep breath and start outlining an unreadable cursive on his chest. "One of the families I used to live with would bring people over. I never saw them because our caretakers would shove all five of us into a two-by-four closet and lock the door. With chains." I snuggle closer to his warm body. "We would be in there for hours and when someone would finally open the door, our caretakers would be passed out on the couch, and the whole house would smell…funny. As I got older and more knowledgeable about the world around us, I realized they had multiple addictions, and meth was their favorite party favor." I chuckle a bit, but purse my lips when I realize a tear is falling from my eyes. I've never told anyone. Not even Lily.

I remove myself from Rowan and sit on my knees, facing him. His hand reaches out to mine and his thumb rubs circles around my palms. "This scar is from my father," he says. I place my other hand on top of his. "He has anger issues. Only threatens me now that I'm older. But as a kid, instead of taking it out on my mother, he took it out on me."

"Rowan I'm—" He shakes his head, cutting me off.

"I'm not. I'm glad it was me and not my mom."

I swing my legs over his, sitting in his lap, and grab each of his cheeks. "You and your mom don't and didn't deserve that." He removes my grip and brings my hand to his lips. I lay my head back on his chest, and he pulls me in tight. I lie there listening to his slow heartbeat until my eyes feel heavy and I can no longer keep them open.

I wake to Rowan leaving kisses along my shoulder and his dick growing into my stomach. I mumble unintelligible words, trying to open my eyes.

"You smell so fucking good," he whispers. His hips slightly buck against my stomach, and I can't help but moan.

I place my hands on his chest, forcing myself to sit up. "How long have I been asleep?"

"About an hour."

"I need to shower," I grumble. My eyes close when I feel his fully hard cock just above my navel. The soreness between my legs reminds me of what has happened today. "And maybe eat."

"I'll make us dinner and save you for dessert."

I snort as I swing my legs over his body, sliding down the bed and start looking for my clothes. My fingers grip through my scalp as I realize I left my phone back home in New York. I haven't spoken to Lily in almost twenty-four hours. She probably thinks Rowan murdered me. "Have you heard from Jace? Or know how long we have to hide out for?" I remember before we left, he said he was sending Jace to watch over Lily. I'm sure on top of her thinking that Rowan murdered me, she's most likely thinking of a thousand ways to murder Jace and get away with it. She hates him more than anything and I'm sure his accent is driving her insane.

Rowan sits up slightly against the headboard, shrugging his shoulders. He is still fully naked, and I can't help but look down at his third leg. When he catches sight of my view, he smirks.

Rolling my eyes, I look away and pick up a towel off the floor. The towel I was using to dry my body off after the shower right before I was ambushed by the greedy pussy demon over here.

"Jace is at your house. I haven't heard from John, so I told Jace to go check on him as well."

"Can I borrow your phone?" He reaches for the dresser, unlocks his phone, and hands it to me. I run to my room, throwing on another dress—one that is too tight, thanks Lily—and dial her number.

As I walk down the stairs, the phone starts ringing.

"Hello?"

"Hey, Lily."

First there is silence. Then hard footsteps, a door slamming, her mumbling, "Oh my god, Celeste." Followed by her screeching, "Where the fuck are you? This fucking Irish lover boy is refusing to leave our house. He said something about you and Rowan having an emergency? Made me pack clothes for you and told me you would be gone for a while. What the fuck is going on?! Jesus, Celeste, when I said go talk to the man, I didn't mean disappear with him as well!"

Actually, her exact words were: *"Go kiss and make up and leave me the fuck alone."* I roll my eyes as I walk out the sliding door to the porch. "I'm fine, Lily. Look, it's a long story but… we are in Italy. I don't know how long we are going to be here for and Jace is there to watch over you. So be nice."

Lily laughs manically. I can already imagine her throwing her head back. "Be nice?" Her voice drops to a whisper. "Celeste, he doesn't say anything to me, just stares. And anytime I tell him to leave, he just… says no and continues working on his computer. But anytime I serve him at the club, he calls me Alan. Fucking Alan! He doesn't even know my name!" She continues going on about her and Jace's experience. I can't help but smile at hearing that a man told Lily "no." No man has ever told her no.

I walk barefoot into the grass, sitting at the ledge in front of the lake. If these people ever catch up to us, at least I was finally able to get out of the States and view some more of the world besides New York and Greece—

"Oh my god, Celeste! Are you listening to me?"

"Yes, I'm here." I shake my head, forgetting I was even on the phone, enraptured by the view in front of me. "Look, I will call you as much as I can. Just don't do anything stupid." *Like kill the poor man*, is what I want to say, but if she doesn't already have the idea in her head, I don't want to be the one to plant it.

"Anything stupid—" I hang up on her before letting her finish. I love Lily, but if I talk to her any longer or tell her what is actually going on, she might end up convincing me to come home and send me a screenshot of a plane ticket.

I set the phone down near me and dangle my feet off the ledge. The sun is setting and a cool breeze flows from the water below.

"Is everything alright?"

I look over my shoulder to see Rowan standing behind me wearing shorts that hang low on his hips, no shirt, and a cigarette in his hand. "You smoke a lot." I turn back around to watch the waves hit the rocks.

"Only when stressed." He plops down next to me and knocks his shoulder into mine. My heart flutters and this time, I may be okay with it. "My mom's family lives here."

I turn to look at his side profile as he continues to stare into the distance. He takes another drag of his cigarette before saying, "They disowned her after she married my father, so I was never able to meet all of them."

"Why?"

"My mother told me it was for business reasons. I didn't understand. I was a kid. But recently I found out something strange. An arranged marriage went wrong. Then she married my dad… I don't know. I don't know if any of it is true or not."

"Have you tried asking your dad? Or tried contacting her family since she disappeared?"

He snorts, smashing the bud into the bricks. "My father won't even tell me the passcode to the front door of our family business after hours. I've sent men here to search for her in Italy." He stands, grabbing my hands in his, and smiles ear to ear. "I'm going to take you to dinner since you also burnt the meat."

Burn the meat? I never burn— Fuck, I forgot to turn off the stove.

CHAPTER TWENTY-FIVE
ROWAN

After dinner, Celeste and I walk the streets of Italy before heading back to the house. I tell her I have some work to do before bed and that I will meet her upstairs. I gave her the option to her own room but when I go upstairs and don't see her in my bed, I can't promise I won't drag her to mine.

I sit down at the dining table, opening my laptop to find over a hundred emails from Harper International. I answer as many as I can, scanning over contracts that Megan sent over. One from Lance regarding setting up a meeting with the council in two days.

I end up replying to all of them and tell Lance to push back the meeting. I open up DWYM, enter my password, and multiple files come up. I rub my hands across my face, heat flooding my veins as I open the new file labeled *New York Incident*.

Notes have already been entered by Jace, breaking down the incident scene by scene. At 10:15 p.m., six guys broke into my house. All of them had fully automatics with full chambers, but no bullets were shot except mine. By 10:25 p.m., all of them were dead. At 11:45 p.m., Jacob & Jacob's arrived at my house. Jacob & Jacob's is a *cleaning service* in New York. It's usually used by the mafia, cartels, etc., but Jacob Travashaw does personal requests for a hefty amount. Jace downloaded the invoice into our system. One hundred and twenty thousand dollars for their services.

I pull up my bank account in Italy and make a wire transfer to my US account, making a note to have Jace go to my deposit box so we can pay in cash.

The rest of Jace's notes are research on all the men. The fingerprints were all burnt off, but he was able to pull hair strands for DNA testing. He broke into the police department's system and found all of them in there. Past criminals. All worked for different mafias around the world.

What the fuck does the mafia want with me?

I scroll down to see a note at 12:30 a.m.:

Jace: Drove down to John's house. No answer at the door. Broke in. Only one couch in the middle of the living room. Looked like a squatter house. Trash and needles on the floor. Broken windows. No sign of John.

I pick up my phone and dial Jace. Once the phone stops ringing, I ask, "His place was empty?"

"Empty," he says in a growl.

"Have you tried calling him?"

"Yes."

"And?"

"He doesn't answer."

Surprisingly, Jace seems awake. It should be pretty late in the night in New York, and I would expect him to spit at me for waking him up from his beauty sleep or some shit. I know he has a *thing* for Lily, so I am going to ignore the thought of why he would be awake at this hour. Instead, I bring my focus back to the issue at hand. John has worked for me for almost two years, and I have never had an issue with him. Now that something serious has happened, he is nowhere to be found? "Was it me or you who hired John?"

It's silent on the other line. Too silent. Am I fucking muted?

"Neither of us. Your father hired him after the Club Opal incident and he just sort of never left."

One year, I had a meeting with a competitor company from Asia at Club Opal. Things got out of hand and next thing I knew, we were on the cover of another magazine.

"COO of Harper International sends the biggest CEO in Asia to the ICU."

The pressure behind my eyes extends at the memory. Mother fucker was talking shit, saying I was too young and dumb to be running a company.

I was in my late twenties, so that was his first mistake. Second mistake was calling me dumb. When you talk shit, you get hit. After that, Asia backed out and Lance thought having a bodyguard with me at all times would keep any additional incidents from escalating. After a while, we all got comfortable having John around. He was no longer just my bodyguard, but a coworker helping with DWYM cases too.

"Find history on John and let me know." I'm ready to end this conversation and put my thoughts on something else. Or *someone* else in particular. "And Jace."

"What?" he mumbles through the phone.

"Be careful with Lily." If he does something stupid that could potentially ruin my relationship with Celeste, I am killing him. I hang up on him, slamming my laptop closed, and run upstairs. I peek into the guest bedroom to see the bed hasn't been touched, and when I walk into my room, I find curls hanging off the bed. My lip twitches into a smile as I sneak over to find Celeste fast asleep.

Rounding the bed, I squeeze in next to her. I grab her hips and scoot her close to me, hearing her grumble at the movement. My hands rub against her body, only feeling lace. My dick twitches and I want so badly to see what is underneath the blankets.

"You took so long," she mumbles.

"My apologies." She smells of honey again. Leaning into her neck, I start kissing her, feeling her pulse quicken under my lips. She turns to me and I gently kiss her and wrap my arm around, palming her sweet, juicy ass. When I squeeze it a little harder, she parts her lips, inviting me into her. Our tongues fight for dominance, and since I don't like to lose, I roll her over, getting on top, and place my hands on either side of her head. I feel her hand reach out and cup me through my boxers. She works her way inside, bringing my cock out.

Her hand comes to her mouth as she darts out her tongue and licks her palm before stroking my dick.

This woman is mine.

It doesn't take long for me to cum all over her. I have to admit any touch Celeste gives me can make me cum, but I don't stop there. I like to give just as much as I like to receive. I kiss my way down her body until my head is between her legs. I will never get enough of her. I want to wake up with the taste of her lingering on my lips. I want to see her smile every day. I want to be the one she comes home to. The one who makes her laugh, the one she cries to, vents to, and I want to be the person who takes all her pain away and makes her feel better.

Before I know it, Celeste's thighs squeeze around my head, telling me she's at her climax. She arches her back and gasps for air.

Fuck, I want to see this sight every day.

I roll over to lie next to her, both of us panting. She rolls to her side, slicking her hair from out of her face. "Any news?"

"John is missing."

The moonlight casts a shadow over her face, showing me the concern written in her eyes. "What do you mean missing?"

"Jace went to his house. It's completely empty except for a couch."

She sits up on the bed, criss-cross, and my cock twitches, ready for round two at the sight of her breasts bulging out of the lace bra.

"I thought he lived with you?" she asks.

"John?"

"Yeah."

"No. Why would he live with me?" I can count on one hand the number of people who have permission to step inside my home, and the only person who has slept at my house besides me is sitting right in front of me.

"Well, because the night I stayed over… he was there. Sitting on the couch downstairs when you were sleeping."

I think the vein in my neck just popped. My whole body freezes and it feels like I've been violated in so many ways. Uncontrollably, my breath picks up and it feels like fire is coming out of my nose.

"Rowan?"

I stand from the bed and start pacing back and forth in the room. The only time anyone is allowed in my house is when I need them to be in my house. The only time I need John in my house is when I call him to come to my house. How would he even get inside? I have never given him a key.

"Was he not supposed to be there? I figured he lived with you on duty or something. I don't know. I'm sorry."

I stop pacing and turn to face Celeste, seeing her now standing on her knees. "Never be sorry. I just… I don't know how he got in the house." A nasty taste lingers on my tongue. Is this what failure feels like? I have failed my mother and now I'm failing at my business. People getting onto my property, entering my property without my knowledge?

"Your employee who is supposed to protect you doesn't have a key to your house?"

"No, of course not. I don't need protection." I continue pacing back and forth in the room.

"Then why did you hire him?"

"I didn't… Lance did." I stop. Lance hired him. I did no background check on John, just accepted my father's conditions and let John follow me around.

"Your brain is on fire. Would you like to fill me in on what is going on in your head?"

Biggest Fan

Turning to Celeste, I see her arms crossed and her nose scrunched. I walk back to my side of the bed and get underneath the covers. I lean in, giving her a soft kiss on the forehead, and stare up at the ceiling, contemplating committing mass murder.

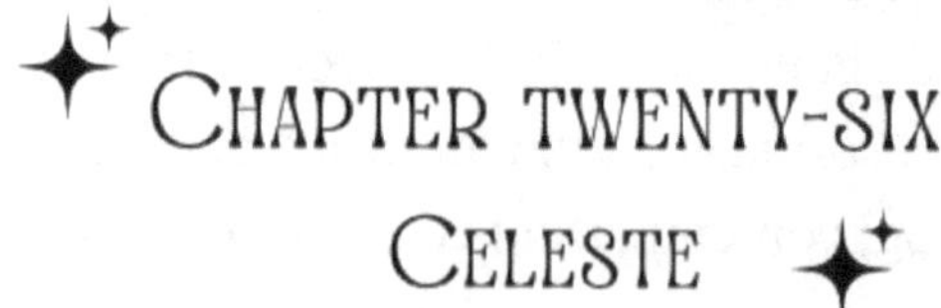

Chapter Twenty-Six
Celeste

I walk down the stairs hearing Rowan's yells turn to whispers, then to growls. He never told me what the issue was last night. John gave me the creeps when I found him sitting on the couch that night, but I thought nothing more of it. He's a bodyguard—he was body-guarding, or whatever.

When I round the corner, Rowan's eyes shoot up from his laptop, looking like he did not sleep at all last night. He has a slight beard growing in, and his hair is longer, touching the tips of his ears and sweeping further down his forehead. I wish I could help him solve all his problems.

He hangs up the phone, closes his laptop, and walks over to me. Grabbing me by my waist, he kisses my forehead. "Good morning."

"Good morning," I shoot back, giving him a tight smile.

"I'm going to get dressed and take you through the rest of Italy. I believe there is fruit and some orange juice in the fridge if you're hungry, but we will be stopping for food." He rubs his hand along my arm, walking past me and up the stairs. Any touch he gives me makes me want to never let him go.

Thankfully, I had one normal outfit in my luggage. Jeans and a T-shirt. Unfortunately, the only other shoes Lily packed me besides heels were my damn flats. After hours of walking, I would not be surprised if my pinky toe is permanently crooked with a missing nail. At the end of the day, it was all worth it. The food was amazing. Bloat from pasta, what? Never heard of that symptom. Plus, the biscotti, cannoli, and all the breads, butters, and jams my heart could desire. Rowan even taught me something in Italian. *"Faccia de cazzo."* He won't tell me what it means, and when I repeated it, all he did was laugh.

The streets were packed this time of the season, and by the time we got to Venice, the high tide rolled in.

As soon as we get back to the house, Rowan starts working on his laptop on the dining room table and I go into the backyard to soak up the sunrays, listening to the waves crash and the birds in the trees.

"Buonasera."

I open my eyes, nearly falling from the lawn chair to see someone standing above me. An older woman with long black hair, dark eyes, and cheekbones that Tim Burton would die for.

"I'm Alessia. You must be Celeste, it's so nice to meet you." She reaches her hand out, but after everything that has happened, my fight or flight mode kicks in. Who is she? Why is she here? How does she know my name?

I turn around to look through the sliding glass door and when I turn to look back at her, she is staring at the door as well, right at Rowan.

"*Perdonami*, I'm Alessia, Rowan's aunt. I doubt he has told you 'bout me though." She smooths down her dress and picks up a brown bag before walking toward the house. I quickly follow her as she lets herself in.

Rowan immediately notices our uninvited guest and stands from the chair. "Alessia. What are you doing here? How did you know I was here?"

"*Cazzone*, your mother never taught you anything, huh?" Alessia says as she walks toward the kitchen and drops down the brown bags on the island. She takes a deep breath and looks between the two of us. "Why did you never tell me your wife was so beautiful?" She stalks toward me, rubbing her hands across my shoulders and down my arms. I tense in response and Rowan takes a large step closer to the both of us.

Wait, did she say wife?

"Because the family excluded me the day they learned I was alive," Rowan says between his teeth.

"*Sei così ingenuo, figlio mio.* Sit down, I brought carpaccio." She waves us off, walking back to the kitchen and emptying the brown bags. Turning around, she opens all the cabinets in the kitchen until she finds the plates.

Rowan takes my hand, guiding me to sit. "Should we be worried?" I whisper and Rowan only responds with a shrug.

Rowan

I've only ever seen Alessia in photos my mom showed me. I would have never expected her to willingly visit me, let alone know where I would be staying.

I carefully watch as she stalks around my kitchen, preparing us all plates. "Are you going to tell me why you are here?" I ask, no longer able to play this bullshit, friendly-fake, family game with her.

She sets the plates down in front of us. Neither Celeste nor I move.

Alessia takes the seat in front of me, clasping her hands on the table. "As soon as you tell me how far along you are."

Celeste wiggles in her seat. And in response, I just glare at her, not having any idea what the fuck she is talking about. Is she pregnant? Is this some type of women-telepathy shit? I release some of my tension when I feel Celeste's hand grab mine under the table.

Her mouth opens, but Alessia cuts her off. "The investigation, Rowan. How much do you know? Did your mother ever tell you about the Messinas?"

I bite down on my tongue, not understanding why I feel such grief. I should be relieved that I misunderstood what Alessia was asking, but for a moment I imagined what my life would be like with Celeste and a kid.

I may have panicked for a second, unsure if I'm ready to be a father, but what I am sure about is that I love Celeste and I would love our kid.

"Hello? Rowan?" Alessia snaps in my face to get my attention.

Messina is my mother's maiden name. "Why would she? You guys disowned her when she married Lance." The tension in my jaw triples as soon as the sentence leaves my mouth.

"That's what she wanted you to believe."

I grip Celeste's hand a little tighter when I feel her about to leave. "I feel like I shouldn't be here for this," Celeste says, but I pull her back down to sit while still staring at Alessia.

Alessia looks at Celeste and gives her a tight smile. I feel like jumping over this table and strangling her with her pearl necklace for even being in the same room as Celeste. What kind of family member, flesh and blood, completely cuts off their connection to their sister?

"Joan only left us because of your father. Lance forbade her to ever come back home."

"Why?" I snap, the back of my teeth clenching with enough pressure to crack a tooth. I can see Lance doing some stupid and misogynistic shit like that, but if it's true, I need to know why.

Alessia's chest enlarges as she takes a deep breath. "Joan got involved with a man named Max. She fell in love quickly and didn't know what she'd gotten herself into until she was at the altar. Our whole family was there, including Max's family, the Rossis. Once she realized what she got into, she left. Never came back. She ran off with your father, got pregnant, and had you. Your father's business sky rocketed. He got greedy and wanted more, so he got in touch with the Rossis and your mother disappeared." Alessia leans back in the chair, crossing her arms over her chest. "And then you go chopping off the heads of the Rossi family!"

"I may have done some questionable things to a man named Max Hinderburg." I squint my eyes at Alessia, trying to keep it PG in front of Celeste. "You're telling me his name was Rossi?"

Alessia nods her head in confirmation.

"How do you know what I may and may not have done?"

"Streets talk."

I promised myself I would never get involved with the mafia. Jace and I had offers, knowing the people we know. But we both always refused. But here I am, killing them off like cockroaches. I can feel Celeste's eyes staring at the side of my face as I continue to look straight forward.

"Look, your father told you a lot of lies to keep you hidden. But congrats, Rowan. You killed Max Rossi and now have the whole family and their goons on the hunt for you. And because you are here, I'm assuming the last hunt didn't go so well. But what I am really here to warn you about is John. He was sent to kill Lance long ago, but somehow Lance got out of it and Joan disappeared at the same time." Alessia's eyes go glossy and fuck, I believe her. And fuck me for not knowing my own bodyguard's last name.

I clear my throat. "Who is John?" I ask as a trick question to see if we are talking about the same person.

"John. The man I see standing behind you in all the photographs online."

I scratch at my neck, feeling like I'm being violated all over again. I turn to look at Celeste. Her jaw has dropped and her eyes are wide, staring back and forth between me and Alessia.

"Why are you telling me all this now? You know I have been searching for my mother since day one."

"Because as soon as word got out that Max was dead, raids were happening at the Messina households. Don't worry, we can handle ourselves."

I wasn't going to offer help.

"Joan started the fire the day she ran from the altar. Lance added the wood. But you, Rowan, you poured gasoline and are standing right it."

I sit back in my seat, nearly pulling my hair out of my scalp.

"Find out why Lance is still alive. John was supposed to kill him. And look closer at your mother's paintings. I could never decipher them, but she always hid messages. And when you find her, let me know so I can smack her on the back of her head, *facia de cazzo*." Alessia grabs at her necklace, twirling it between her fingers before she stands from her seat and leaves without another word.

"The fucking mafia!" Celeste jumps from her seat.

"The fucking mafia," I repeat.

Chapter Twenty-Seven
Celeste

I make circles around the kitchen counter mumbling, "The fucking mafia" multiple times. Rowan disappeared upstairs instantly after Alessia left.

The fucking mafia.

I'm really trying not to make this a *me* thing, but we are talking about the fucking mafia here and I need a plan as of yesterday for how to get out of this alive. If I would have kept my ass home, none of this would have happened. How in the hell does a small-town foster child, wanna-be artist, get herself into this mess?

I take a deep breath. Think, Celeste.

No thoughts come to mind. Only fear.

I head out of the kitchen to go talk to Rowan. He might be the only person who can calm me down. As I make my way through the living room, I stop when I remember what Alessia said when she left. *"Your mother always hid messages within her paintings."* I look back and forth between each painting. There are four in total, one on each wall.

"Rowan's mom, if you can hear me, I mean no disrespect," I say as I take down all her paintings and place them on the floor. I stare at the puzzle in front of me, noticing that there is one color present across each painting: a deep hazel blue applied thickly on every corner. I start putting the paintings together until—

"What are you doing?"

I turn around to find Rowan walking down the stairs with our bags. He stares at me in confusion before his brows scrunch together, his eyes reaching the floor.

"It's a bell inside a jar. Does that mean anything to you?"

"What?" Rowan continues down the stairs, leaving our bags at the bottom of the steps. He stops in front of the paintings, his mouth opening and closing as he stares at the art. He creases his lips and turns away. "We need to leave now." Grabbing our bags, he walks out the front door without looking back.

It was a quiet journey back to New York. We sat in silence—like always—the whole car ride to the airport and the only time Rowan spoke to me was when he advised me that he hired someone to watch over me and Lily until things settle.

I didn't argue. I did, however, feel useless. Maybe he didn't see what I saw in the painting. Maybe it meant nothing.

When we land back home, he drives me to my house and walks me up the stairs. Before I even have a chance to open the front door, Jace runs out and down the stairs like he couldn't wait to get away. When I turn around, Rowan leans in, placing a kiss on my forehead, and follows Jace out into the street, back to their cars.

I stand in front of the door, feeling the abyss of emptiness crawl into my skin. Nausea creeps around the corner.

Until I'm tackled from behind by a linebacker. "Oh my god. I'm so glad you are home!" Lily's wet hair smacks me in the face as she wraps her arms around me and drags me back into the house.

We sit down on the couch in the living room for over an hour as I update her on everything that has happened, feeling more comfortable telling her all of this in person rather than over the phone. From the start of the story—me ambushing Rowan in his house and dragging him to come take photos with me as a paparazzi—all the way until Alessia left the house in Italy.

"The fucking mafia!" Lily screams.

I sink further into the couch. "Yeah, the mafia." I rub my hands into my eyes, now realizing how tired I am.

"Don't worry, Celeste." She puts a hand on my shoulder. "I'll protect you."

"I love you so much, Lily, but how would you—" My eyes widen when she reaches behind the couch and pulls out a gun. "What the fuck, Lily?! Where did you get that? Do you even know how to—" Before I even finish my sentence, Lily does something to make the weapon click. She points it toward the kitchen and pulls the trigger.

I duck and shoot back up, looking to see where the hell she just shot. My eyes squint as I look above our kitchen to see a target taped to the wall above our cabinets. I run up to it, pulling myself up on the counter to see there is no hole in the wall. But down on the counter is a small rubber ball.

Lily walks up behind me. "Like I said, I can protect us." She gives me a wide smile. "Jace..." She stops her sentence and looks away. "Taught me."

"Jace taught you," I repeat, smirking at her already knowing where this is going.

"Yeah, these past couple of days were kind of hell having him in the house. We fought a lot."

"Mhm." I lean my hip on the counter, crossing my arms.

"He bought me this gun and taught me how to use it."

I lift an eyebrow and I can see the nervousness radiating from her body.

"Anyway," she sing-songs. "I took the week off and I heard you quit your job. So let's party!"

I roll my eyes, remembering *I* didn't quit my job. Jace quit my job. And now I need to find a way to come up with money *again*. And fast.

"Well, maybe not party, since I have school," Lily continues, "but we have a lot more free time! Oh my god, let's go to Club Opal."

I shake my head, waving her off, and walk toward my bedroom.

CHAPTER TWENTY-EIGHT
ROWAN

"What the fuck, Rowan!" I stand in front of Lance with my gun shoved into his forehead. Jace is by my side with his Glock pointed at Lance's chest. When we broke into his house, we found him passed out drunk on his couch. I've been poking at him with the barrel of my gun for the last five minutes.

"Care to explain the Rossi family?" I dig the barrel deeper.

"Get that fucking gun out of my face."

I grab him by the collar, standing him in front of me and moving the gun to his temple. "You're such a fucking coward, Lance." My blood starts to boil as I stare into the emptiness of his eyes. He has no heart. No soul. He is a body bag filled with nothing, caring for no one but himself.

"I saved your mother," he spits.

"Saved her?" I retort, pushing his plump body back onto the couch and letting out a manic laugh before scratching my head with my gun. "She what, left the altar for you? Ran from the frying pan into the fire?"

"Oh please, you're so dramatic, Rowan. Always have been. Your mother was going to raise you as a pussy. I raised you to be a man."

"Well, here is the man you raised, Lance. He is standing right in front of you with a gun pointed at your fucking face. I don't care if you are dead or alive. You've never been my father."

"Then what is holding you back? Pull the fucking trigger if you're such a man."

"Ye don't even want to explain what happened?" Jace asks at my side.

Lance looks toward Jace and snorts. "I did business. That's what happened. Something you kids will never understand."

I'm not going to hold back anymore. I'm tired of being overlooked.

I smash my gun on the side of his head. Blood flies out of his mouth all over his precious couch. He wipes it away with the back of his hand. "You and Jace are fucked. I hope you know that. They will come for you! And better watch out for that little whore of yours. What's the bitch's name? Cel—"

I slam my fist down on his face before he can let her full name come out of his filthy mouth. He looks back up to me with a bloody smile.

"She sure did have a fun time running around New York, jumping into anyone's car, thinking it was a taxi. How was Greece, by the way? I should have given my man something stronger. She sure is tough."

Red fills my vision. I slam my fist down again. Grabbing him by the shirt, I throw him onto the floor. Again and again, my fist cracks into his face. I hear his bones split and the smell of iron fills the room as crimson runs down his face and onto the floor.

My knuckles go numb, but I continue beating him. Not wanting to stop. Not going to stop until his eyes sink into the back of his skull and his brain explodes through his ears. I feel the pull on my shoulders, but I ignore it.

"Rowan!"

I'm shoved off him, Jace's arms completely wrapped around my ribs and landing me on the floor. I shove Jace off me, staring at the possibly lifeless Lance Harper.

Jace picks himself up and places two fingers on Lance's neck. "We will never get any information from your father if he is dead."

"He's not my father," I say as I walk out the front door.

CHAPTER TWENTY-NINE
ROWAN

Jace and I stand on the other side of the street as I watch Harper International catch on fire.

Room by room. Floor by floor.

Glass shatters and falls twelve stories down.

We went through the building, making sure nobody was inside, then threw down multiple gallons of gasoline on the top and bottom floors. I lit a cigarette while we exited the building, inhaled a couple of puffs, allowing the burn to numb my lungs, then threw it down on the floor.

I never wanted to walk in my father's footsteps, let alone take over his business. I tried doing what is right by him and our name. Instead, all he ever did was drag me, my mother, and our name through the dirt.

We wait a few minutes before jumping back in the car to go to Lance's house. I know he is still alive. Evil never dies. So, I will enjoy beating him until I get all my answers.

I filled Jace in on everything before getting back on the plane to leave Italy. He's been around my family for so long, he has taken my situation to heart. He runs the red lights and swerves between cars going well over the speed limit as I pull up the DWYM program, researching John Rossi.

I find him on a street camera two days ago at an ATM in Cold Springs, hiding right under our noses. "Head for Cold Springs."

"What?!" Jace yells, gripping the steering wheel tighter than before.

"I found John, head for Cold Springs," I reiterate. I brace for impact when Jace makes a U-turn in the middle of the intersection.

We came to the closest motel we found near the ATM. After a little fake flirtatious chat with the assistant at the front desk, I was able to get information that a man named John Wilbur is in room 306.

With one kick, we slam the door open, Jace and I pointing our guns and looking around to find John in the corner of the room, a gun in his lap and a toothpick in his mouth. "Took you long enough." His once flawless English accent has dropped and the Italian in him explodes like acid from a bottle.

We both keep our guns up. Jace walks to the side, closing the door and heading to the window to shut the blinds.

If this is my demise, I'm haunting Celeste for the rest of her life. Not out of hate, but out of regret. I should have tried harder. I should have said more. Should have told her how I really feel. Flashes of the times we have spent together run through my head like a marathon. The weapon falters in my twitching hand.

John stands from his chair, placing his gun on the nightstand. "You boys put the guns down and take a seat so we can have a conversation like real men."

My finger itches to pull the trigger. Jace drops his arm, but I keep mine pointed. "How are you related to Max?" My barrel follows John as he walks to the mini bar. He pours liquid into a cup and takes a small swig.

"He was my nephew."

"Fuck," Jace whispers, running his hands through his hair and pacing by the window.

"You helped me... kill your nephew?" I say as I lower my gun. "Why?"

"Technically I didn't help you *kill* him. I helped clean up," he says nonchalantly. "I took over the family business once my grandfather died. Max couldn't help but want in. He knew the business. He got caught. He paid the price."

My head pounds between my eyes. John runs the Italian mafia, and he was working for me this entire time. I run my hands through my hair, now pacing the room. Jace sits down on one of the twin beds. "You run the mafia, but you have been following me around for years, acting like my employee. Why? What deal did you make with Lance?"

"We wanted Joan home. My nephew wanted his *wife* back. We kept our eyes on Joan for a long time before Max picked her up. You know how we are with our women. We pick them and we breed them until we are finished with them." John shrugs his shoulder and lights a cigar. "The deal I made with your father is that we take Joan and he doesn't die. But what we didn't know was that Joan was already missing. Your father said that you were searching for her, so I decided to stick around and see what you find."

What the fuck is happening? And what the fuck did he say about women?

I try to take a deep breath, feeling like a hundred-pound weight is on my chest, leaning against the wall for stability. "Well, the deal is off, you can go home. Joan is dead." I look at Jace, who finally shoots his head out of his hand, staring at me with wide eyes. That is the one part I left out of our conversation. I didn't want to tell him until we finished business.

Alessia was right, she did leave a message for me, and Celeste was the one who found it.

John rubs his hands down his suit and tie. My skin goes from ice cold to lava hot, crushing the gun in my hand. I could blow a hole right between his eyes for thinking my mom is some type of handbag he can just buy and give away. If I kill him, how many other people will I have to take out until the whole Rossi family is nothing but dust in the wind? A forgettable memory?

"Well, if that's true, then your father is a dead man. We made a deal. We get Joan and he gets to live."

I shrug my shoulders, not feeling any type of remorse for Lance. "If you don't do it, I will," I whisper. I'm sure Lance is long gone by now, probably in another country.

"Why haven't you killed us?" Jace questions.

John starts packing his bags, grabbing a gold ring that lies on a dresser. "Don't worry, boys. This ain't over." He smiles, walks out the door, and leaves Jace and I to ponder in the dark.

CHAPTER THIRTY
CELESTE

I had a pregnancy scare thanks to Rowan's aunt. Both me and Rowan misunderstood her when she asked, "How far along you are." I got anxious, and Rowan got clammy. Fortunately, she was talking about the investigation. Unfortunately, I haven't been able to ignore the fear that I am. I tried to ignore it since my doctor told me it was almost impossible, but I kept having debilitating cramps, and I wasn't sure if it was my PCOS or if I was really going to have a baby. Therefore, I took a test as a precaution.

Then another.

And another.

Thankfully they all came out negative, because I haven't heard from Rowan in months. He doesn't respond to my calls or texts. The last I heard was his family's business burning down. If I had to guess, I'd assume he is the one who did it. I've decided that, after my sixth text message and third unanswered call, I would leave him alone.

It has created an empty hole in my chest, knowing that he is somewhere out there, possibly still looking for his mom. The only way I know he is still alive is by searching the internet every day for deaths in Italy and New York. I scan the county's obituaries every day and stay up to date with the news.

It pisses me off that he's not answering me. I was dragged into this, became invested in his life, and now I've been dropped like I am nothing. What ticks me off even more is now that I have no contact with him, I miss him. I miss him like I've known him my whole life. He crawled his way into my brain just like he said I did to his and it's driving me insane. Every time my phone vibrates, I pick it up hoping to see an unknown text or call and it be him. Everywhere I go, I smell his cologne, thinking he is right behind me. Stalking me. Watching me.

Lily told me she lost her job at Caffe Latte, but since it's so close to Central Park, I still stop by here to grab my coffee. I try to keep my mind positive and not hyper fixate on the Harper family. In light of everything, I ran into someone at the park who needs an artist for her first exhibit. I showed her my social media, and she immediately said yes. Now, with my free time, since I don't have a stable job—as if being a paparazzi was stable income in the first place—all I focus on is my art.

I sit in one of the corner tables by the window, planning out all my artwork to show. It's a gloomy day outside, the weather at its shittiest since we came back to New York. I'd do anything to be sitting outside again underneath the Italian sun.

I peek my head up from my notebook, noticing someone standing right in my peripheral. "Can I help you?"

"Celeste Jones?" The woman standing in front of me is wearing knee-high boots, dark worn out jeans, and a big leather coat. Her pin-straight black hair swivels from her shoulders down her chest, and her smokey eyeshadow is slightly smeared.

"Yes?" I whisper.

She quickly pulls out the seat across from me. I close my book and place a hand on my bag, ready to run. "Hi, I'm Sasha. I don't know if you remember me but—"

"Sasha!" I lean across the small table. "Holy fuck!"

"I know." She pushes her hair back behind her ears and removes her coat to hang on the back of her chair. "I'm so sorry if this is odd, but I got an email, and it's been so long I had to come."

"An email?"

She smiles, interlocking her fingers on the table. "How are you, Celeste Jones?" She stretches her arms out to me. "You look good, girl. Living out here in the big city. What do you do now?"

I lean back in my chair, noticing the empty café. The new barista is only paying attention to her phone. "I'm good. An artist just trying to survive. What do you do? Do you live out here?"

She gives me a faint smile. "I'm here and there. Do things... here and there." I cross my arms over my chest, squinting my eyes at her, and she laughs. "It was hard for us growing up. After you left, it was just me and the boys. We did what we could to stay alive."

I uncross my arms, reaching for her hand on the table and giving it a squeeze. "I wish it was different for us. I'm sorry I was taken away."

I have nightmares about that day, our foster mother nearly yanking me back by my hair because I wouldn't let Sasha go. Us running together and trying to lock ourselves into the bathroom. The boys throwing glass from the cabinets, screaming to leave us alone. That mother was one of the worst, saying things to us, smacking us around, treating us like her personal maids. But me and Sasha took it together. Then you add the boys and they made the mother's life a living hell, only making things worse for us. I knew the boys would take care of Sasha when I was gone, but it didn't make it any easier for my heart knowing I was leaving. I wonder if she has the same PTSD as me? Small spaces, deadbolts…

She slides her cold hands from off the table and sits back. "Wasn't like it was your fault."

I swallow the bile stuck in my throat. "That email... Did it come from Rowan Harper?" I have to ask. Sasha looks like she's in a business she's not supposed to be in. And a busy café nearly cleared out in two minutes right when I find her standing in front of me? I have searched for her before, not finding any social media on her. It was like she disappeared from the earth. Now that I'm involved, or *was* involved, with someone who can find any person on this planet, she randomly shows up? It can't be a coincidence and I'm not stupid.

"I can neither confirm nor deny." She winks.

That mother fucker.

"I don't have much time." She snatches my pencil and notebook, turning it her way, and finds an empty page. "I want to catch up more. Just another date." She slides the book back my way and stands from her seat, sliding her coat over her shoulders. "It was really good seeing you, Celeste Jones."

I look at her scratchy handwriting. A number with the letter "S" underneath. My eyes water as I watch her through the window. She walks past the building and disappears into the crowd.

Chapter Thirty-One
Celeste

"Come on, Lily! We are going to be late!" I quickly slap on some lipgloss and run my hand over the black velvet dress. The train in the back was longer than I asked for and once I saw it, I immediately panicked. Once one thing goes wrong, everything else falls apart. And if this train gets stuck underneath my heel, and I trip and fall, I will personally execute myself in front of everyone at the exhibit.

"I'm ready." Lily steps out of her bedroom in a tight, short black dress and—

"Is that Louis Vuitton?!" I bend down to look at the heels. "Was I sleeping or something?! When did you get these?" I look up at Lily when she takes a step back, her face turning into a strawberry.

"Um... from a friend," she says, biting her bottom lip. "Now come on, we are going to be late. It is your big day!" She grabs my hand as we run out of our house and call for a cab. If we are going to be late, it's her fault. She took two hours getting dressed and asked me multiple times which shade of nail polish she should wear.

I can feel my back sweat as I think about how many people are going to be walking around and staring at my artwork. Judging. I spent dozens of hours, sweat, tears, and late-night bowls of ice cream on these paintings and I'll be damned if I hear a negative review.

I stop at the door of the gallery, rubbing my clammy hands along my dress. Lily turns to me, grabbing my shoulders. "Nobody is in there right now, babe. I promise it's going to be okay. If people don't like your artwork, then I will personally shove my foot up their ass."

I look at my reflection one last time through the glass windows and turn to Lily. "Why would you ruin your Louis Vuitton?" She smiles and pulls me through the door.

Last minute details are happening— balloons, waiters preparing drinks—as the DJ plays some quiet music.

The girl I met at the park, Alecia, claps her hands and throws them in the air, swirling in her heels. "Girl, this is awesome! Look at your work!" She hugs me and pushes me back by the shoulders. "Let's sell some motherfucking art."

Alecia opens the door a few minutes later and a stream of people flows in. People I did not see lined up outside. The DJ turns up the volume as the building starts to flood. I try to keep my balance as I watch everyone come in. This is more than I expected, partially thanks to Lily since she decided to invite her whole law school. My cheeks are burning from smiling so hard. I don't know if I am supposed to talk to people, introduce myself, or stand in the corner like a wallflower.

A microphone appears in my vision. Alecia hands it to me. "Make your speech."

Speech? Speech?! Nobody said anything about a speech. I hesitantly grab the mic and Alecia walks away. The DJ turns down the music and somehow, all eyes are on me.

"Hello." I bounce from putting my weight from one foot to the other. "Thank you everyone for coming tonight. This um... show is a mixture of my life and others'. My goal was to show people that at any time, our bubble that we secure ourselves in, can be popped. And that in any moment, the lid to our jars can be opened. And when that jar opens or that bubble pops, you may find... love, happiness, or peace. But you may also find darkness, greed, and hunger. Either way, good or bad, it's okay to remove our lid and pop our bubbles, because you may just find what you love and who you love.

There are certain paintings, if sold, whose proceeds will be donated to the foundation listed below the frame." Someone woos in the far back, making me smile. "I hope everyone has a great time." I hand Alecia the microphone back and the crowd claps before dispersing.

I take a deep breath and scurry to the wall in the middle of the building to stop at my favorite painting yet, *The Jar*. It's the view of Rowan's lake house. The lake is below a velvety blue sky, the mountain smeared purple and pink and sitting in the middle of the water. But sitting right at the ledge, on top of the brick wall, is an open jar.

"This one is my favorite."

I quickly turn around at the dark tone in my ear, seeing Rowan Harper standing behind me.

I want to be angry. I want to yell at him in front of all these people, but when my eyes start to burn and my hearing becomes muffled, all I can do is wrap my arms around him.

I've missed him.

I try to gather myself, sniffling the tears back and wiping my hands down my dress. "I'm sorry to hear about your father's business."

"I'm not."

I squint my blurry eyes at him and he smirks. This little arsonist did do it.

"Did you..." I'm hesitant to ask. It may not be my business to know anymore. Rowan disappeared for over a month without a word. His feelings for me may have changed. But I need to know if Rowan finally got his peace. "Did you find your mom?" I whisper.

His eyes turn dark, his lips flip down, and in
that moment, we are the only two in the room. I
watch as his chest enlarges and deflates.

"The Bell Jar, by Sylvia Plath. You solved
her note, Celeste."

I shake my head. "I don't get it."

"It was her favorite book she would read all
the time." He walks around me, getting closer to my
painting. "As a kid, I used to watch her read it in her
room at least once a month. One day, I asked why
she always read that one. She told me, 'I aspire to
be like the author.'"

"I-I still don't get it."

He chuckles, turning around to face me
again. "I didn't either. But as soon as you found the
note, I did a quick search on the author to find out
she committed suicide."

I cover my mouth before I reach for his
hand. "So you think…"

He nods his head. "I know."

I still have so many questions. How? When?
But all I can do is shake my head. "Rowan, I'm so
sorry." This was not what I wanted for him. This is
not what I expected.

He pulls me into my chest, holding me tight.
"You helped me find her. I got my closure and
that's all I need." He pulls me away, holding me by
my shoulders, and wipes his thumb across my
cheeks. Wiping away the tears that I hadn't realized

I let drop. "Today is not about me, though. It's about you and I am so proud of you."

Well, he might as well rip a hole in my chest and take my whole heart out himself. "Wait," I say, patting at my face, hoping I don't have makeup streaks down my cheeks. "Did you send Alecia to find me?"

"Why would you think that?" He gives me a tight smile.

"Because you found Sasha." I narrow my eyes. I swear, if he set this whole thing up, I might punch him. I don't like to be a violent person, but I might just do it. And then kiss him. Because if it wasn't for Rowan Harper, my jar would still be closed.

"I can neither confirm nor deny any of those statements." He pulls me in closer and kisses me on the forehead. "I love you, Celeste. And I am your biggest fan. I would do anything in the world for you."

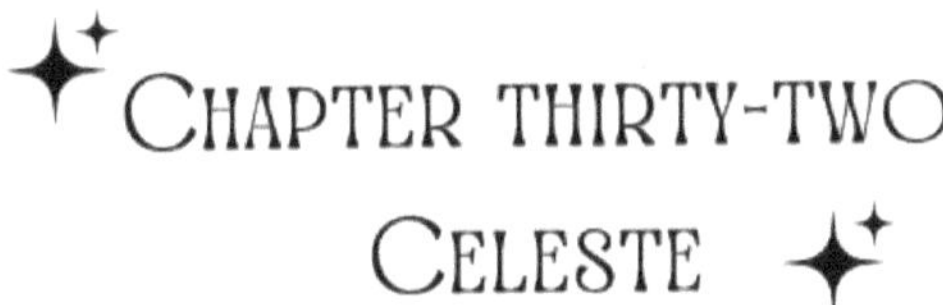 Chapter Thirty-Two
Celeste

Two months later...

"Girl, are you sure about this?"

I put my hands on my hips and tilt my head to the side. "I'm only moving in." Bending down, I throw more brushes I found underneath my dresser into the box of miscellaneous items.

"Yeah, but you do know, once you move in, then comes a baby and then comes a wedding," Lily says.

I laugh and shake my head, taping up the box. "I don't think that is how the saying goes." I look up to find her eyes glassy, her lips pouting, and I swear if she cries, I will cry. Lily and I have lived together for years. She has been at my side through everything, and I am so grateful for her. "Lil, I swear. Don't you cry."

I hold out my arms for her and she bursts into tears, running toward me and wrapping her arms around my neck. "I just want you safe."

I know I will be safe with Rowan. I trust him, he takes care of me, and he has become my everything. He may drive me insane, but lord help me, I love that man.

I smile when I see him leaning against the bedroom doorframe.

"You know, Lily, we have an extra room. You can come stay with us and drop this nasty house," Rowan says.

Lily backs away from me, wiping at her tears. "Ew, gross. I do not want to hear you guys have sex every night." She places her hand on her hip and points at Rowan. "I swear, if you do not take care of her, I am going to break into your house and strangle you in your sleep with a shoelace."

I snort when Rowan ignores her, walks toward me, and kisses me on the forehead. He picks up the box I finished taping and walks out the door. "I can continue paying my half of rent so you don't have to find a new roommate," I tell Lily.

"Oh god no. You're a grown-up now. Go live your life." She smiles, "I have to grow up at some point. Or I'll just find someone else to tell me when to eat and sleep. Oh!" She pauses, picking up tape and working on another box. "Maybe I will find me a professional chef to be a roommate."

I can hear her choking on her words again, so I open my arms, and she runs to me for a second time. We may still be living in the same state, but it won't be the same and I am going to miss her. She also better take note of all this hugging because she has used up her allotment for the year.

"These are all of them, yeah?"

Lily's body tenses around me, and I pull back, finding Jace holding a box. His eyes bounce to Lily and quickly look back at me. I peep at Lily to find her hands in her shorts pockets, looking down at her feet. "Yes, those are it. Thank you." Once he leaves, I turn to her and pinch her arm.

"Ouch!"

"Did you guys fuck when I was in Italy?" I whisper.

"What?! No!"

I shake my head. She's lying. They definitely fucked. He must have finally learned to pronounce her name correctly. I giggle to myself as I grab my purse and walk out the door.

I find Rowan standing at the moving truck. "Ready, heaven?"

I roll my eyes and smile. "Are you ready? Are you sure you want to do this? You know I like to blast music, throw paint around, dance naked..." I wiggle my brows. There's a lot more I can do to destroy his bachelor pad.

"I know. I love to watch you do all those things." He grabs me by my waist, pulling me into a kiss.

"Stalker," I say, slapping him on the chest.

"You stalked first." He winks at me and smacks my ass when I hop into the truck. I wave back at Lily through the window. As the truck drives off, I watch her frame through the side mirror, seeing her still standing outside and looking at Jace's car.

My life has changed since the day I met Rowan Harper. I've seen things I can't unsee. I've run from people I thought I would never have to run from. Since I was a kid, I've felt as if I've never truly had a family. But when Rowan reaches over and intertwines his hand with mine, I know that I have finally found my family. And I have a feeling that this isn't the end of everyone's story.

Thank you for reading

I appreciate you for giving this book a chance. As an indie author, reviews are extremely important, and I would not be able to thank you enough if you were to leave a review on Amazon or Goodreads.

FIND ME ON:

Instagram: @authoramaia
TikTok: @authoramaia

Preview

Curious on what happened with Jace and Lily while Rowan and Celeste were in Italy? Keep reading for a preview of the first chapter of *Biggest Regret*.

Chapter One

Lily

I swear, if this stupid keyboard goes out one more time, I'm tossing it out the window. I look at my bedroom window, remembering it is nailed shut. Okay, never mind.

I hang my head over my desk chair, staring at my ceiling while spinning in a circle. I have a test due in two hours. I haven't eaten since… oh I don't know, yesterday? I have my notes scattered along my desk, and I can't see the floor in my room due to all the open books. Every time I turn on my computer it gives me some type of matrix coded program, as if I'm some kind of computer wizard. I continue to distract myself by counting the number of holes I have on my ceiling. It should only take a couple of minutes before my screen is back up and running.

I stop spinning my chair when I hear the doorbell ring. I tap my phone screen to see it's 10 a.m. I shake my head, getting out of my chair. The only person who could be ringing the doorbell at 10 a.m. is none other than my best friend, Celeste, who I will be murdering for running away last night to go make up with her boyfriend and not tell me. I mean, I did tell her to go kiss and make up, but *she could have told me she was going to go kiss and make up,* instead of having me sit at home all night worrying my ass off.

"Forget your keys, did you?" I shout while walking to the door. I unlatch and unlock all the deadbolts I installed and swing the door open. I squeeze my eyebrows together, putting my hands on my hips. "What are you doing here?"

I thought it was Celeste at the door because she left her keys, but no, fucking Jace is standing in front of me looking like a deer in the headlights. I watch his eyes dart from my legs to my face, then look back over his shoulder. I scan my own body, noticing I am only wearing boyshort underwear and a tight tank top my breasts are overflowing out of. I've worn this exact equal amount of clothing in the club, so I don't know why his cheeks are flaming red as if he has never seen me like this before. I slam the door in his face since he is taking too long to answer my question.

"*Álainn,* I need you to open the door."

"No thanks. You have the wrong house!" I yell through the door.

"Lily. Open. The door."

I place my ear to the cold wooden frame. "Why?"

"It's about Celeste."

I open the door, peeking my head out. "What happened? Where is she? I swear, if you guys killed her, I will murder you and your entire family. I watch murder documentaries. I know how to get rid of a body. All you need is—" Jace shoves the door open, forcing my body into the foyer table. "Hey! Excuse you! I did not say you can come in!" I kick my front door shut and follow him down the hallway and into my kitchen. He sets his laptop on the counter and drops a duffle bag on the floor.

Oh lord, he is here to murder me.

Oh, you're still here? What a good girl. Here is
your reward…

Bonus Scene

Rowan

"I think I'm the luckiest man in the world to wake up and have heaven right beneath my covers," I whisper into Celeste's shoulder, my hands roaming down her back until my fingers grip her thick thighs.

"Rowan, please," she moans. "We don't live alone anymore, remember? Noah is right downstairs."

I can't help but groan, throwing the blankets over my head and leaving kisses down the side of her hips. Having Noah in the house will never stop me from fucking Celeste. And when her hips splay open, allowing me to taste her sweet pussy, I know her previous complaint doesn't matter to her either.

I move her panties to the side and lick up her cunt, savoring the sweet and slightly salty taste of her morning pussy. A breakfast I can feast on for the rest of my life. Her legs spread wider and I mumble, "Good girl." Wrapping my arms underneath her thighs to bring her even closer to my face.

My dick is being crushed into the mattress, but I don't mind. I'd do anything to continue hearing the sweet moans fall from her lips. The more I suck on her nerve, the louder she gets. The wetter she gets. All for me. Her nails dig through the blankets above my shoulders as I suffocate between her thighs.

"More," she begs. Always been my needy girl. And when my girl wants something, I make sure I give it to her.

I push the blankets off, picking her up to sit her on my cock. Her mouth pops open as I fill her to the brim. Her arms hang over my shoulders and she rolls her head back, letting me suck and kiss across her neck.

"I'm so sore," she states, but continues to roll her hips, her slickness dripping down my balls.

"But you can take it, can't you?" With my arms wrapped around her back, I try to pull her further down. I know there's no more dick left—all eight inches are deep inside her—but if I could crawl into her skin, inject myself into her, I would.

This is us every morning.

Having sex.

Making love.

Fucking.

And since she has moved in, my life has been nothing but happiness. I don't care for the world around me. I don't give a fuck about anything but having Celeste at my side.

Her moans vibrate in my ear, causing my dick to twitch. I lay her on her back and thrust into her until her moans turn to cries. Her eyes slam closed and her back lifts from the mattress. With her legs shivering at my sides, I know she's about to come. I pick up one of her legs, stretching it into the air and laying it over my chest, the angle allowing me to feel how tightly her pussy is squeezing my cock. When she doesn't let up, I come inside her, making sure she gets every last drop and pushing as far as I can inside her.

I thrust one more time for good luck, smiling at her when she breaks her eyes open and squints at me. "You're a menace," she says, trying to push me off.

"I'm not done," I tell her, trying to grab ahold of her wrist when she rolls off the bed. She snatches the blanket from underneath me and wraps it around her body.

"Oh, yes you are! I didn't even get to clean up from last night!"

I pick up my shorts from the floor, catching her at the door. I flip her around and crash my lips on hers. "Tell me you love me."

She smacks her hand on my chest. "Yeah, yeah."

"Tell me."

"I love you," she says and kisses me before she quickly flips around, giggling and running down the foyer to her art room.

I jog down the stairs and when I look up, I find Noah *and* Jace at the bottom of the steps.

"Jesus, ever heard of boxers?" Noah snaps.

"Nobody asked you to be here." I flip him off.

What once was a silent home has turned into a fucking clown house. But they're family.

My family.